I am Those Women

Cruz Galdón

I am Those Women

First Edition: 2022

ISBN: 9781524318314
ISBN eBook: 9781524328306

© of the text:
   Cruz Galdón

© Layout, design and production of this edition: 2022 EBL

To my father, who kept these stories and the memory of these women alive, and to my children, because this story is also your heritage.

Table of Contents

Chapter I
Time To Undress

Bellavista de la Jara, 1910.

"Armando, here is your son. His name is Samuel. Unfortunately, we weren't able to do anything to save his mother. Natalia has passed away. Are you going to bury her in Puerto de Santa Maria?"

So, that is how Samuel Almena, scion of a family with ancient roots, came into the world. They were landowners and potentates of the time when wealth was measured by estates on which cattle ranged freely. Their pastures stretched across the Sierra Morena, where pedigree bulls with stamina delighted matadors and gentlemen alike. It was a time when farms made money from raising cattle to fight in the bullring and breeding swift horses that could outpace all others.

Samuel was an only child, who being motherless, grew up with his father and grandfather. Capricious, elegant and extremely attractive -his looks more Anglo-Saxon than Andalusian- his eyes were an intense and attentive blue, the kind of eyes which said it all when they looked at you. His blond hair was the color of wheat, thick yet soft, and always well combed. His father always said that a good coat, and good shoes always polished, made a man a gentleman.

But what am I doing? I started with the birth of Samuel, and I didn't even mention where this whole story took place.

Bellavista de la Jara, the principal town of the region, is in Andalusia, at the beginning, or end, of the Sierra Morena; a town whose citizens had lived there all their lives, as had their ancestors before them. I read not so long ago that the very first settlers surpassed those ancestors in weight and stature. But how do you compete with an archosaur of the Mesozoic Era?

It is certainly nice to see that what children now visit as ichnite footprints, in Samuel's time, was the orchard of Uncle Nicasio. There the protagonists of these stories went to bathe in the pool, pick delicious blackberries and play on the threshing floor where they had a thousand and one adventures. And those cavities in the rock were simple hollows. But now it turns out that those hollows, where the children made mud pies, are in fact dinosaur footprints.

It's true. Bellavista de la Jara was home to dinosaurs fleeing the ice age. They settled here, before my Iberian, Roman, Visigoth, Arab and Christian ancestors.

It is a place surrounded by three mountains that act like three loving mothers embracing their people: San Roque Hill, El Castillo and La Guardia.

Samuel grew up like everyone else who lives off rents. He studied as much as he wanted, and was shaped by his class, his ancestry, and the standards of the time. With his father, he went to the fields and learnt how to check that everything was in place; that the bulls were all they should be and that they were prepared for fighting in the second and third class bullrings and, on two occasions, in the Las Ventas bullring in Madrid. How I loved, as a girl, to go with you and my father to the bullring! How serious your countenance, which wanted to convey all the intensity, nobility and prayer that each set of bullfights meant for bull and bullfighter!

"Samuel, your father is calling you. Go to the casino, he's not in a good mood and I don't know what's upsetting him."

"Marcial, it won't be that bad. Probably just some game that has not been to his liking or someone spat on his beliefs and values. You know how the Master always rants."

"Samuel, hurry up! I don't think it's going to blow over."

It wasn't far from Samuel's house to the casino, but you had to pass through the square, where the young women were filling their pitchers, and filling the morning air with chatter and gossip, along with the occasional stolen glance at men and boys passing by.

Samuel arrived at the square, adjusted his jacket and hat, looked at the time on his watch - twelve noon - took a deep breath, lit a cigarette, and then put his silver lighter in his pocket and walked briskly to where the girls were.

Samuel thought, "This Angela, my God! This brunette robs me of my senses! Such olive-green eyes! And how they pierce my soul! She's driving me crazy! But how can I get close to her when she is just the shoemaker's daughter?"

"Good morning to you, fair damsels, and may you all have a good morning."

"Good morning, Master Samuel," they answered in unison.

"Consuelo, how is your father doing? Come, I have something to ask of you. I'm giving you this errand discreetly because all of these girls prefer gossiping to breathing. When you see that Angela is alone, tell her that I'll pass by her window today, so she should be on the lookout for me. I've been wanting to talk to her for days but I couldn't find a time or place. And when you have told her, without saying a word to anyone, come straight to the casino where I'll be with my father. When you give me a signal, I'll be right out."

"Yes, Sir. Be assured that I'll be as discreet as possible."

The casino was in a corner of the square. By leaning just out of the door, one could make out the fountain, the girls, and the horses tied to the town hall building. But, from the window located to the right of the door, where the Almena's table was, the view was complete without the need to move. Through it, Emilio could see his grandson's movements, his gestures and the pouts that made him so dashing that his grandfather could almost feel himself young again and strutting among so many beautiful and helpful girls. But he was worried. He knew of the feelings that had captured his grandson's heart and that they could not bring anything good, that brunette having the father she had.

"With your permission, father, grandfather," Samuel said, taking off his hat and bowing slightly, addressing his father, Armando, and his grandfather, Emilio. "Marcial said that you wanted to see me about something very important, so I came at once."

"Samuel," said grandfather Emilio, "your father is worried about a rumor that concerns you which is being spread in these parts. You know, son, that you are the bastion of this family, that your deeds bring both honor and dishonor, and that the Almena estate is sacred. Soon you will have to choose a wife from Demetrio's daughters, from those of Doña Dolores, or from the surrounding area, but you must choose with sound judgment, prudently and with clear vision. Living off the rents is not simple in these times; besides money attracts money. Do you understand me, Samuel?"

"Father," said his father, Armando, addressing grandfather Emilio. "Stop beating around the bush. This rich brat, who is my son, is making a fool of me and I will not allow him to laugh in my face for one minute more," he said, staring at his son. "What is going on between you and the shoemaker's daughter? Gossips tell me that you are serious about her and that you are sending her a message to court her. Don't you realize that you are going to be the laughingstock of the whole town? That her father is on the breadline and an anarchist free-thinker! For God's sake, Samuel, he doesn't even have his daughters baptized! Isn't that enough for you to stay away from such company?"

"Father, why do you say that? Don't talk about Angela like that!" Samuel answered in a choked voice.

"I'll speak as I please and as my status permits me. You are an Almena. Neither your grandfather Emilio nor I ever had dalliances with just anyone in our entire lives. And that girl's family is nothing. Look how her father struts about being the priest's best friend. Debating the divine and the human for hours and hours, as if his deliberations were the fruit of the most erudite of philosophers and theologians while in reality he is a puppeteer and organizer of mockery and farces for the amusement of the town. Open your eyes, Samuel, for God's sake. I'm glad your mother isn't here to see you... she was a true lady! Now, listen or...."

"Father, I beg you not to keep talking like that. Don't offend me. Angela is the most chaste, good, simple, dignified and beautiful woman I have ever known in my whole life. I have loved her from the very first moment I saw her; from the very first moment her big almond-shaped eyes fell on me. I just want her to be at my side. Father, for God's sake, don't keep making a fuss about something pure and sincere."

Don Armando stood up and, resting his fists on the table, gave a blow that silenced everything, the click of the domino tiles, voices and glasses in the casino. All those present were waiting to see what would happen next. Samuel took a step back. Grandfather Emilio tried to speak, but Don Armando intervened,

"Be quiet, father. If this ingrate marries that woman, given whose daughter she is, from that moment on, let him take note that he is no longer my son and that he can forget about getting a single coin from this family. You already have what's yours. Think and reconsider. That woman is not worthy of your ruin. Now get out of here."

With such a love, the whole of life yields to that feeling; the heart is channeled and nothing else enters but air and enough food to survive; it is the immense passion that marks the rhythm of the soul's heartbeat.

Which would Samuel choose? His class and estate or the love of his life? That first love that enters without asking permission and hunkers down, filling the whole of his being: his thoughts, his joy, his stomach? This was a serious crossroads for a young heart who at barely seventeen years old is being forced to choose. How can you deny loving freely and with an open heart to such a young son, for the simple and unfair fact that the object of his love belongs to a low-class family with different beliefs and opinions, when Angela did not even know how to read or write?

After the quarrel, Samuel disappeared all day with the excuse of going to the countryside. He saddled his horse and galloped away from the town, crossed the threshing floor and reached the road that led to the farm. Two phrases repeated over and over again in his mind: "My dearest Angela" and "I'm sorry, Father".

When he arrived at the farmhouse, the poor horse was bathed in white saliva from its bit. Its body was sweating and its mane was tangled by the strong April wind, which had wreaked havoc on the horse along the roadside. He climbed down from the horse and handed it to the stableman and raised his arm to gesture that they give it food and water. He went to the huge kitchen and saw the water jug that bore his initials and which perennially sat on the slaughter table. Lifting it up, as if it were a trophy, he let the fresh water run into his mouth, over his chin and his chest, but it did nothing to refresh his soul, which burned with the thousand emotions that tormented him.

"I love her so much that my chest hurts; and if I lose her, I don't want to live anymore. But my father says I must, and also my grandfather, whom I respect and love so much. What will become of me without his protection and advice?"

The night fell pitch black. The sky had filled with clouds and the wind swayed the leaves of the olive trees. The estate's hemp harvest was still growing and a hailstorm or an extreme west wind could endanger it all. The animals, restless, stirred in their stalls and Samuel, wondering what to do, dithered between keeping his date with Angela or letting everything die.

"If I don't return to you, I will lose what I love most in this world. But if I love her more than anything else, what am I doing wondering what to do? I must leave quickly if I am to meet her. But what if my father has found out, or sends Marcial to watch the cobbler's house? Did my father not learn what it's like to lose the love of his life? Father's soul was ripped apart. That's why he hates me; that's why he won't accept my happiness. That's right, he doesn't accept that I'm happy because I killed my mother at birth. I'm sure he blames me and that's why Grandpa Emilio always comes to my defense. That is why he moderates the sharp blows my father inflicts on me with his words.

If I go, I will be with her forever. If I stay, cowardice will be the mainstay of my existence. I will have chosen money and position over the love of my beloved and dearest Angela.

Meanwhile, in Bellavista de la Jara, things were afoot that would dash Samuel's hopes. In life, sometimes by just moving a single piece or setting up a situation, you change what happens. Thus Marcial Marchena, Don Armando's right-hand man, went in search of Consuelo, Samuel's confidante.

"Consuelo, go by the Bodegones House, Don Armando Almena has sent for you, and he says to be quick about it."

"But Marcial, why does that curmudgeon want me to go there? Besides, after the hornet's nest he left in the casino, there wasn't a man that wasn't shocked at how he talked to his own son. Don't count on me, man, that old guy's got it in for me for going to Angela's house as a matchmaker. No way!"

"Consuelo, either you go, or I'll take you by the hair. If they call you, you go and that's all there is to it."

It took a long time to get from the hermitage where Consuelo lived to the Bodegones House, and it was not because of excessive distance, but rather because of the number of slopes that had to be traversed. With her tongue stuck out and cursing her luck, Consuelo arrived at the Almena's house with Marcial Marchena.

"May I come in?"

"Yes, Marcial, the master is waiting for you in the courtyard."

The courtyard of the Bodegones House was large and rectangular with a wooden portico, the roof of which was covered with huge vines full of bunches of grapes waiting for the summer to ripen. In front, on both sides of the stables, there were two enormous fig trees that were the delight of young boys at dawn, and of some gentlemen who, before going to urinate, would drop by to savor a tidbit.

The principal room, in the north wing, overlooked the courtyard and had large aspidistras and ferns that made it the coolest place in summer, and there, in his bulrush armchair, Don Armando Almena placidly smoked his pipe after lunch.

"Come in, Marcial. Is Consuelo with you? Send her in."

"May I, Don Armando? I'm here because you Marcial said you wanted to see me. What can I do for you?"

"Pay attention to me with all your intellect, little as it is. Go to the cobbler's house and tell his daughter that, if she loves my lad, she should stay away from him. There's no one knows better than she that she's not good enough for my son, and that it's not to my liking that they continue conversing. Moreover, if she really loves him, she will do as I ask. In return I will send them food so that her father will be more comfortable."

"Anything else?" she asked, tight-lipped and clenching her fists.

"Yes, two things: that this message will leave your mouth just once and that will be to its recipient; and that the medical assistant will come to your house to see what your father needs. That way you will be well paid for the errand and for your silence. You can go now."

Marcial and grandfather Emilio looked askance at Don Armando. They could not believe the extent to which he was willing to involve himself in his son's life. The two exchanged sad and disapproving glances at the lousy decision he had made. They bowed their heads and each one, as though they were on separate paths, went to different places in the Bodegones House: Marcial to the stables and Grandfather Emilio to his office, knowing in advance that the chess moves played by Armando were going to lead to a war with too many casualties.

Consuelo arrived at the shoemaker's house angry with herself and with her own mission, for she knew Angela and such scorn seemed to her the worst of sins. "Killing love was like killing a person," she repeated to herself over and over again. And, to top it all off, the errand girl and messenger was going to be her. Fortunately, her father would now receive the medical care he needed so much, and that quieted her conscience a little, but the mean thing she was about to do, and for her own benefit, made her feel miserable, her friend was going to be a poor wretch.

"Angela? Come out, the miller's Consuelo is here to see you."

"Hello, Consuelo, what are you doing here at siesta time? Come in and take a drink from the jug, woman. You're all sweaty and red as if you'd been chased here by the devil!"

"Oh, Angela. I don't know about the devil, but I've just come from his first cousin." She took a long drink of water, which was cool, but seemed like bile to her. Listen to me, because I can't hang about, and it's life or death that I give you the message that I've been sent from the Bodegones House to tell you. You must forget Samuel, for his sake, if you love him. His father tells you to stay away or you are going to disgrace both yourself and him. He says that he'll thank you for doing it by helping your bellies get a little fatter. I can't talk about this with anyone else and in exchange for telling you and keeping quiet, he will send the medical assistant to my house to see if we can heal my father. My dearest friend, forgive me for telling you this and for being the bird of ill omen that has to bring the storm cloud to your heart, but think, isn't Samuel too much for you? What would you do in that big house with so many big rooms and you, a poor ignorant woman? When you are loaded down with children, he will have a proxy and you will be a poor dupe. Listen to Don Almena. Forget about Samuel. Another will come along who will make you a queen! Don't cry, for God's sake! It breaks my heart that you're the joy of this town and that rich kid doesn't even reach the top of your espadrille. Give me a hug."

Angela was not able to hold back the weeping that chokes you, that tears you up inside, that grips your body so you are barely able to articulate any sound other than a sob.

She must have felt she had lost all hope and how, from that moment on, it was up to her to act. Yes, she was illiterate. She did not know how love poems were written, or how to sing to her beloved. She did not know what the taste of a kiss or the caress of a touch was like when one loves so much. She did not know what shivers skin contact produced, nor what it was like to die in Samuel's arms, but she did know what the pain of loving and not being able to love was like.

It was getting dark. The wind brought the echoes of the voices of the oaks closer. As Samuel walked towards Bellavista de la Jara, the reins of his horse over his shoulder, he felt that each step on the path was making the beat of his inner voice stronger. He had decided to go to the window of the cobbler's house, though for exactly what he did not yet know. At times he was the battle-hardened gladiator who didn't give a damn about anything, and the next moment he was secure in the gratifying placidity of his class. Without further thought, he decided to hurry and not delay his destiny any longer.

"Angela, Angela... Are you there?" I'm dying to gaze upon her.

"Good evening to you, Samuel. I didn't think it would be to your fancy to show up at my house on such a cold night. What can I do for you, Sir?"

"Angela, allow me to call you by your first name. What I have come to tell you is the most important thing I have ever said, and since a window separates us, the seriousness of a protocol is not needed."

"As you command, sir, but I don't think it's good for someone like me to be able to talk so familiarly to an Almena."

"Enough, Angela. I'm nobody if you're not by my side. I love you as only a man knows how to love, which is deeply with my whole heart full. And I know, Angela, that you also ardently desire me. I know how you look at me and how you drop the cloth from your pitcher every time you go to the fountain in the square so that I can crouch down and run my eyes from bottom up, until I stop on your face, on that mouth and those eyes, which are the closest thing to heaven. Angela, today at the casino...."

"Shut up, Samuel. Don't go on. I already know what happened today in the casino. The whole town is talking about how your father sent for you to make it clear that I'm a nobody and always will be."

"Angela. I will never let you say again that you are a nobody. You are everything to me and that is enough. You are mine and neither heaven and earth nor inheritance and estate will separate me from you, my dearest and most beloved Angela. Do you get it now?"

"Samuel," she continued, putting her hands out the window to bring them close to his face, "this will be the first and last time I will caress your face. It will be the first and last time I touch heaven; the first and last time I love. Your father is right: I am nothing compared to Miss Adela, or to others like her. My clothes, my hands, my manner of speaking, and so on. I don't know how to read or write. I don't even know how to pray. I don't know how to walk in high heels or how to braid my hair to look like one of those ladies. I don't know how a lady behaves. I don't know how to give orders, because I only know how to obey. I don't know how to embroider; I only know how to mend. I don't know how to cook home-cooked meals, because we only have enough for porridge and an egg now and then; I don't know how to make donuts, because I only know how to knead bread. I don't know how to starch a shirt-front, because I never saw one. I don't know.... But I do know, Samuel, that you will never forgive me for separating you from your father and grandfather. What today seems so easy to you, tomorrow will be my sin. What today you think is not worthwhile, tomorrow will be your yearning. What today makes your blood boil, tomorrow will be the blood that you disdained but love so much. Samuel, come closer. Give me your hand."

Samuel brought his body and hand closer. She took it lovingly in hers and brought it to her heart. The beating was so strong that it resembled the drums of the Easter parades. Her tears spilled over their joined hands.

"I love you and I will always love you, but I will never see you again. Promise me that you will marry and be happy; that you will do your best to honor your name and family name and make a good man of yourself; and that you will forget me. I will help you to do so, Samuel. I swear I will, even if I die inside, because I love you so much that I would never forgive myself if I made you suffer. And, if there is a God, may he know that everything I'm doing I do for love. Goodbye, Samuel."

Angela closed the window slowly, but decisively before Samuel had a chance to say goodbye. He did not understand anything now. He wanted so much to hear from Angela again, but she had closed her window and vanished from the world as if she were an angel returning to heaven. He no longer had anything to decide; everything had already been said; and his love was lost in the air of that inclement April night.

Their destinies had been cut short on that endless night when both were about to wish to die little by little, except that love does not kill but destroys slowly. That night appeared full of misunderstandings between each one and the rest of the world. Both desired the other with all their souls yet were unable to say, "I'm sorry", "Forget it", "It was just an outburst", or "let's throw caution to the winds and run away".

How helpless he felt that third parties had ruined their happiness; and, even sadder that he was accepting it without remedying it. But was it out of honor and generosity or simply fear that Angela was denying herself everything and considering herself nothing?

Angela, while brandishing the principles of honor and generosity, had given up fighting the most important battle of the first part of life, first love.

Who has not pressed his head against the pillow wishing it would come to life and drown his sorrow? Who has not shouted at the sky intoning "why me"? Who has not died today for love, but has to continue living for love tomorrow?

Chapter II
Dressing In a Different Skin

After the window closed Samuel felt that the whole sky had fallen on his shoulders. His heart pounded. There was no possibility of turning back because they had all decided how his life should be. So, he slowly walked away from the shoemaker's house, leaving his heart chained to the window. In her soul she carried all her belongings and because he was no longer in her heart, he no longer belonged to her. But was he really a sentimental person, the kind of person who would let his heart be filled with pain to its very depths?

He let himself be distracted for a while by prized liquor and some not so desirable company. He was looking for his beloved Angela, but she had been swallowed by the earth. No one knew where she was, and if anyone did, they would not tell him her whereabouts. But what could he do to look for her? Where could a humble woman without resources be? He hammered his head again and again, wondering if perhaps she had been sent into service; but with whom? It was unbearable to think that someone could abuse her kindness, her gentleness, that anyone could give her orders and that she would do whatever she was told without a murmur; such was Angela's nature.

The first heartrending days passed without being mitigated by any balm. Little by little, the days of April gave way to the flowery May and, with it, to the festivities of Pentecost: the revered bull runs; the girls dressed up for the festival in their manila shawls and mantles to adore their precious Virgin in Santa María la Mayor.

That time, which he alternated between spending time with his friends and going with his father to the casino, gradually gave him separation and restored normalcy. And it was a Saturday night when he saw in the distance a young lady with a distinctive swing of the hips approaching, who seemed to him to be Venus descended from Mount Olympus.

"Good evening, Miss Adela. You look, if I may say so, really pretty."

Samuel slowly approached her, offering his arm so that she could take it and enjoy a little stroll through the square, allowing himself to be seen by all those present, including Don Armando and his father Don Emilio, who, without a word, said a thousand things to each other in a glance.

"Good evening to you too, Samuel. What a pleasure to see you at the festival. I heard on the grapevine that you were indisposed because of lovesickness."

"Don't be a gossip, Adela! Remember "an unbridled tongue is the chariot of the devil"; such tattle is the product of foul-mouthed girls; and you, I know, are not one of them."

"I'm sorry, Samuel, please forgive me. I found out from my mother, who in turn heard it from my father, who was at the casino that day. I only want to know how you're doing after your breakup with Angela, but I phrased my question inappropriately. Let me try again. How are you feeling, Samuel? You can be honest with me."

"Adela, let's walk together, give me one of your smiles and promise to dance all the paso dobles with me tonight..., as for the rest of it, don't worry about me, my heart is healthy and full of life."

All eyes were focused on the couple. Barely a month after Angela left town, the young man was already dazzling the heart of a beautiful lady. Though it is true that a mulberry stain can be gotten rid of with another green mulberry, Samuel did nothing but live his grief as he pleased, without worrying whether it was the right thing to do or not. After all, they had all decided his life and did not grant him the right to any say.

Adela's exaggerated laughter made all the young girls envy her good fortune to be the one Samuel Almena chose to dance with. Who could wish for more? Her mother swelled with pride at seeing her daughter in the gallant arms of Don Armando's heir, as she counted off each of the four farms he'd inherit.

"Adela, it's time to accompany you to your parents' table. I'll say good night to them, and I'll go with my friends to have one last drink. But I don't want to go without thanking you for this evening. It has been a breath of fresh air in the torment I am undeniably suffering. I didn't answer your question before, but I will now. I am lost, Adela. Without Angela my life has no hope or road to travel. I feel deceived, for everyone has decided, including her, that my love is worth too many farms to deserve her poverty. I did not choose to be my father's son, but so was I born, period. Neither did she choose to be her father's daughter, but so was she born, period. But it is totally incomprehensible and insufferable that they do not let me love. I must be honest; I won't forget her. I cannot; nor do I want to. But neither can I be eternally adoring someone who has closed her heart to me. Despite all this, Adela, I ask if you'll permit me to visit you, from time to time, to get a breath of fresh air. And, if in time you accept me, it'll be God's will."

"I hope so, Samuel. You know I've always enjoyed your company," she said, looking at him, her eyes flirtatious and her voice low.

Adela, daughter of the owners of the best olive and cereal farms in Bellavista de la Jara, was also an only child. She had been schooled to make a marriage of convenience to someone of her own class and, though she had no shortage of suitors, she had always been infatuated, maybe even in love, with Samuel.

Imagine the butterflies fluttering through her stomach as she found herself in his arms, spinning like a top, one dance after another, forgetting time and living in the moment, wishing it would never end. Since she was a rich Cinderella, who had the implicit approval of her parents and was the envy of all her friends, she did not have to leave before midnight and could remain in the embrace of her Prince Charming.

We have all tried to forget the heartbreak of an old flame, but it rarely works. You keep longing for the person you really want to be with. You hate his attitude and even your memories of him; you change your hairstyle, and you even change your clothes; you look for a new perfume; and, in your mind, you repeat a thousand times "I have already forgotten him". Nevertheless, you die inside. If he were reachable, you would give him one of those epoch-making speeches, reminding him of everything he has lost. Spurned and scorned, you keep quiet and concede, and unconsciously look for similarities in the next green mulberry to silence the screams of the broken heart.

I guess Samuel did the same with Adela. It would be his balm and his oasis in the desert of his feelings. His feelings towards Adela were not like those he professed for Angela, which, in a way, made her feel a special and protective tenderness towards him. What would be her role in this saga? Well, surely, to rebuild Samuel's fortitude and to be the one to stem his tears.

The following weeks went by with a moderate degree of calmness and joyfulness. Adela and Samuel took walks around the square and attended the functions of the wealthy families of Bellavista. They even went horse-riding on the pastures, where they could breathe the late scent of spring that was almost summer, letting themselves be seen by anyone who wanted fresh, juicy gossip to share for their personal entertainment. Day after day, Adela hoped that Samuel would take the next step and start using her first-name and perhaps even steal a kiss, but it was an empty dream and, little by little, she began to languish. She knew that Samuel would soon be leaving for his military service, and it was her objective to begin their formal courtship before he left.

One afternoon, while sitting in the rocking chairs in the large living room of the Medina's house, Adela got up to serve her father and Samuel a glass of wine and to order the food to accompany the drink. When she handed Samuel the glass, she gently brushed his hand with such delicacy that a shiver ran down the back of her neck. She looked sheepishly at Samuel thinking he might have noticed her embarrassment and quickly moved to her father's side to appear genteel.

Samuel stared at the glass and his hand, as if Adela's furtive touch was still there. Though he had felt her emotion when she touched him, he felt nothing except the memory of Angela when, from behind the window, she sheltered his hands in hers, wetting them with those tears that he would have drunk to the last drop in order to make his pain and the cause of it disappear.

Samuel thought, "What am I doing? Adela doesn't deserve this. I don't feel a pure and real love for her. I don't feel anything like what I feel for Angela, but maybe she could be enough for me and, if she is content, I will love her in my own way. They say that touching leads to affection, but though she has managed to make me hold her in high esteem, I neither love her nor desire her. Only you, Angela."

"Samuel, you seem distracted. Is something wrong or is something troubling you? Is it because of something that my beloved father or I may have mentioned?"

"My dear Adela, don't think badly of me. Sometimes my mind goes blank and it evokes thoughts about the past, or future, that disturb me. Don't in any way feel awkward about this. It is only a thought."

Adela looked at her father with shining eyes, excited, knowing that what Samuel was thinking was not what she wanted, that he had not perceived that shiver and that she had only evoked a memory. At that moment, her father got up and went to the door, and looking at his daughter blatantly gave her a conspiratorial wink.

"Samuel, I would like to talk about us. I know that it is not a woman's place to discuss these matters but seeing that you are not capable of formally courting me, I need to know what your intentions towards me are."

"Adela, don't you think that this is a matter that should always be dealt with by a gentleman and not by a lady?"

"Samuel, stop being so formal and be intimate for once."

"Adela...," Samuel was silent again. As he remembered how he had asked Angela to call him by his first name, his words reverberated in his head. And now it was Adela, who in an authoritative way wanted him to do so. "It is difficult for me to do that, because I have the highest respect for you. I do not want to, nor should I. I cannot do anything that would be detrimental to you in the eyes of others or myself."

"That's enough, Samuel! Stop beating around the bush. Can't you even be honest about this? You're playing with my feelings just to pass the time until you forget that shoemaker's daughter. What is wrong? Is it that you don't think I'm much more ladylike than she is? Is it perhaps that because of my position and wealth, you don't feel you have anything to sacrifice? Or is it just that you think I'm less of a woman than she is because I'm not a servant?"

"Adela, you have gone too far. I hope you are able to reconsider what you said and take it all back, because you have really offended me. I hope that your words are just a woman's jealousy and that you are not so bold as to want to be the one to decide what and when we have to be. That's a man's duty! I don't like your attitude. I'm leaving."

"Samuel, please don't go. I'm really sorry, I shouldn't have said anything. I should wash my mouth out. Please, I ask you, forget I said that. For God's sake, I can't live without you, can't you see that?"

"Adela, give it a rest. I'm leaving, because I have to think."

What a situation! Both loving madly without its being reciprocated; trying to love to forget, believing that there are no more possibilities or any future. Men and women are at odds, no matter how many years go by, because of mixed feelings.

Adela was in love to the core and ready for anything. Even to the point of being the one who threw herself into Samuel's arms to win an "I love you" from him, no matter how slight, and that might be enough for her…, but she knew it never would be. She wanted the same love that Angela had had; she wanted it all, even though she knew it was impossible. So, she would settle for what she could get: halves or crumbs rather than lose him.

And for Samuel, what a labyrinth of passions, the entirety versus the not-quite. He felt that his manhood and virility did Not allow a woman to manipulate his feelings, let alone reproach him for not loving her as she wished, by imploring and begging him to begin a formal courtship.

Angela, humiliated and hurt by being despised as a lowly daughter of a *persona non grata* for the Almena family, decided, with the help of her family, to leave Bellavista de la Jara as soon as possible.

And so, it was. That same night, after closing the window and telling her father and siblings what had happened, they sought a remedy for her ills. With everyone's agreement, she packed her cardboard suitcase with those few things that her sisters and friends lent her, the small mirror from her alpaca dressing table, unglazed at the handle, and the companion hairbrush with which every night she untangled her braids; the fan with one of its ribs cracked that Consuelo gave her for her sixteenth birthday; the lace petticoat that her sister wore when she was asked for her hand; the white Sunday blouse; the small shawl and the cloak that Señora Carmen gave her to go to mass with her and be baptized; so many little things that fill a small suitcase and seem like a lifetime. Thus, with tenderness and sweetness, she was gradually packing her little trousseau, folding each thing with such care and, as if it were the most precious jewel, in each fold a new tear.

The next morning, with her eyes swollen from crying, her heart at half throttle and the kind of grief that cancels out all crumbs of happiness and hope for living, her brothers took her to the railroad station. It was full of people: ladies dressed in their most elegant clothes and carrying summer umbrellas; carts full of vegetables and animals that were going to be loaded into the third-class carriages; stray dogs sniffing everything.

"Angela, remember, you mustn't get off until the last stop, and as you don't know how to read you will have to be very attentive and ask the conductor. Don't talk to anyone. You are very stubborn and think that everyone is good, but they are not."

"Don't worry, Miguel, I'll be careful, because I will be very attentive and I won't daydream."

"Angela, are you carrying the bag that Fermina prepared for you? It's a long way to Cordova and you'll be hungry and thirsty. It's not a lot, but it's sufficient for you to get to our sister Severiana's house."

"Miguel, don't worry. It's enough. Besides, I have no appetite or thirst, or anything like that. I'm sure I'll have plenty, don't be afraid."

"Sister, this is the best thing you could have done, so don't trouble yourself or brood over it anymore, because otherwise your eyes will dry up and you'll be ugly. If I catch that Samuel, I'll tear his brilliantined head right off, that's what that rich kid deserves. And don't worry about his father, I'll throw it in his face when he goes to Uncle Pedro's oven to get his freshly baked bread, and I'll make it bitter on purpose, I swear on our mother's grave!

"Miguel, don't talk like that about Samuel or Don Armando, they are not our enemies. It is simply not my place to get close to a person who is my better. I dreamed and let myself be carried away by my heart without paying attention to my head; like Eve, I picked forbidden fruit and now I have to leave my Eden. Don't do anything rash or confront anyone. On the contrary, if you see Samuel, hold him in esteem, because he will suffer more than me with so many evil tongues lashing him over everything that has happened. And don't tell anyone where I have gone, because he is more than capable of looking for me. You don't know how persistent he is. How many times did I tell him not to come near me? And how many times has he tried, always with the dropping the cloth trick? If I didn't drop it at his signal, he would throw it away himself. I am anxious, we'd better say goodbye and I'll look for the carriage."

"Angela, you don't know which one it is. Wait, we'll take you to it".

Miguel and Augusto took her to the third-class carriage. The smell was overwhelming: the stink of unwashed bodies, chickens, sheep and even pigeons. She took a seat and arranged the snack that her sisters and Consuelo had neatly prepared for her and placed it with great care on her cardboard suitcase. She even had a hard-boiled egg, butter cake and wine donuts, what more could she wish for? Well, surely a lot more, such as not having to leave her village.

A woman with a sour face took the seat next to Angela, her headscarf highlighting the poor woman's ugliness and Angela's beauty. For an instant Angela forgot her woes and concentrated on the woman's enormous nose and the formidable hairy wart that set off her upper lip. Her thought was none other than; "Goodness, how ugly that woman is."

The bitter moment came. Her brothers embraced her and reminded her again of each and every piece of advice the shoemaker had given her before she left home, encouraging her to be strong. They said goodbye to each other, and she drowned in tears that sank into her belly.

There was a cloud of steam and a deafening whistle as the stationmaster's voice thundered the order, "all aboard!" and as the train pulled out of the station, she knew that one stage had been brought to an end, and she would now have to wear a different skin.

Chapter III
It's Time To Be a Chrysalis

Angela looked out of the train window. After four hours, the jolting on the hard wooden seat made her kidneys ache, especially when - wouldn't you know it - she had started the 'curse'. She, like every other woman of her time, was not able to talk about her daily concerns, because it was inappropriate and uninteresting. Besides, it was the men who dominated knowledge and information and they were hardly going to discuss 'women's issues.'

The point was that one way or another, Angela found herself aching not only in her heart but also in her body. She had prepared as best she could for the journey, but would it be enough? During the first few hours of her departure, she thought about everything that had happened in the last few days and how her life had changed overnight.

"Why me? What did I do to deserve this? Why must I go away? If I am nothing, why go to such lengths to keep me away from Samuel? And now, what is the life that awaits me? What am I to do? Damned love that changes lives so that you cease to be you and become a puppet! I am like a drab rag that is used and then thrown away; but the truth is, Samuel didn't use me or throw me away; I was the one who closed the window. The anticipation of living with my sister and her husband grips me with fear as I have no way to pay for my keep and so I'll be a burden to them. But I shouldn't worry, I'll find domestic work in some big house, no doubt. My sister is doing well and I'm sure she and her husband will find me a good position in service...".

The train stopped again, and her ethereal thoughts ceased, refocusing her on reality. A hen was poking holes in the basket of her fellow traveler. Angela was disgusted to think of how the hen, after pecking at everything in her path, was tampering with the basket of food her companion was carrying. She imagined the hen being the ugly woman's best friend, talking to her about the newspaper and both eating from the same bowl. "I think I'm going crazy. I'm already imagining absurd things, but it seems so real that maybe it could even be true."

"Excuse me, ma'am, there's a... a chicken eating from your basket."

"What was that, girl? Ah! The hen is mine. Her name is Benita, and she always accompanies me. When I go to my brother's house in Andújar, I take her with me. She's so good that she eats out of my hand. I'd even give her kisses if I could."

"Oh great! It's true that the hen eats from the same plate. Well at least I'm not crazy, but now I'm a witch and a fortune teller!"

"What are you saying, girl?"

"Nothing, nothing. Let's hope we get there soon."

The conductor passed by announcing: "next station, Cordoba". They had already arrived at the destination. Her heart began to beat so fast it almost came out of her mouth. She did not know whether to get up to get her suitcase down or stay seated; whether she would have to stand for a long time; whether she would thank heaven for arriving; or whether she should stay seated and not say a word. After a few minutes the train stopped, and she saw fellow travelers get up and decided to join them.

"Good evening, miss. Can I help you with your suitcase?"

"Don't bother, you're very kind, but I can manage it. Thank you."

"It's no bother for me. I don't have any luggage and it'd be my pleasure. My name is Juan."

"Angela. Don't worry."

"I won't. I've been watching you the whole trip and you didn't get up once and only exchanged a word with the lady with the hen. I imagine this is the first time you've traveled alone."

"Sir, excuse me. I'm tired and I don't talk to strangers. I just want to get off and find my family who are waiting for me."

"I didn't mean to upset you. I can imagine how tired you must be and your desire to get to your destination. Let me get your suitcase down for you."

"All right. Thank you."

Angela got off the train accompanied by Juan, which did not please her sister Severiana, who was waiting anxiously on the platform. Seeing her sister accompanied by a young man was not a good start.

"Angela!"

"Severiana, Antonio!"

"My God, I'm so happy to see you!"

"Sister, thank you for welcoming me into your home. I never thought I would have to leave the village, but I have suffered misfortunes, and when we get home, I will tell you about them in private. Oh, Severiana!"

"And who are you?" demanded Severiana, who was a tough cookie. "Give me my sister's suitcase!" she ordered.

"Begging your pardon, ma'am. My name is Juan del Rio and I'm studying medicine. I don't really know your dear sister, but I offered to help her off the train. If you would permit it, I would like to see her again."

"Thank you for your gallantry and excuse me, but we are not here to greet you. We hope that your work comes to fruition and that you have a good stay in Cordoba."

"May God bless you, ma'am, and you, Angela, and grant me the miracle of being able to see you again."

Severiana and Antonio had been married for five years. He worked as foreman on a farm on the banks of the Guadalquivir and she was the housekeeper in the farmhouse. She was in charge of keeping the farmhouse in perfect condition for when the gentlemen came out to the countryside and held parties and gatherings for poets, musicians, singers and other members of Cordoban society.

It was getting dark when they arrived at the farm which was called La Serena. The smell of the fields and the humidity of the river on those April nights made Angela feel cold. She squeezed her sister's arm and snuggled into her shoulder. She closed her eyes and remembered, from when she was a child, the smell of her mother, who would hug her and give her a kiss on the forehead. As if her sister was able to read her thoughts, she kissed her forehead and caressed her hand.

On arriving at the farmhouse, Severiana took Angela to the kitchen, gave her a bowl of hot broth with a splash of sherry to warm her up, accompanied her to her room and helped her unpack her small cardboard suitcase. In that moment of solitude, the two embraced each other as only two soul sisters do. Then Angela broke down. She related through inconsolable tears how Samuel's love had arisen, how he had courted her and how Don Armando Almena had forced her to leave his son. When she had to narrate how they had said goodbye, grief did not allow her to continue. Severiana silenced her with a kiss and taking her with both hands, consoled her.

"You are safe now, my girl. Everything will be alright, you'll see; you'll forget your grief here. Your love will be cast aside and then you can return whenever you want. But don't think about that now. I only want you to feel free to do what is best for you. You know father always taught us that, even as women, we are free to decide what we should do with our lives. His freedom of thought made us equal to men, whatever it may seem to some."

"Severiana, I am not free in anything. I am a poor wretch who is despised for being who I am, the daughter of a shoemaker."

"I won't let you say that again. We are the daughters of parents who love us; a mother who loves all of the seven children she bore, and a father who worked his hands to the bone making shoes to give us a crust to eat. Don't be ashamed of who you are. You are special, Angela. So special, that you make people next to you dream, and their thoughts soar when you tell your stories, so much so, that the all the girls in the neighborhood want to be like you. Even the posh ladies envy you because Samuel Almena fell in love with the shoemaker's daughter."

"And what good is that to me, Severiana! Look at me. I'm like a limp rag. I feel like I'm dying."

It was a night of confessions; one of those endless nights in which the arrival of sleep is prevented, despite intense fatigue, by fear that the ghosts of the broken heart will use memories to poke at the raw wounds and break the heart even more.

The days of May arrived and with them, the gaiety of Cordoba. The floral crosses showed Angela the beauty of the Cordoban patios, and the houses decorated with flowers, little by little colored her heart.

At the beginning of her stay, she helped her sister with the housework. She loved the smell of lavender in the closets and the clothes that her sister so lovingly ironed. She loved how her sister handled that key ring with hundreds of keys, knowing which one belonged to which room and how she gave orders to everyone without restricting her mandate. If she had to give orders, she would die, she only knew how to obey.

On Sundays, she wore her white blouse and her sister brushed her long hair and taught her how to braid her black hair differently. Then it was time to go to mass, after which they walked around the Jewish quarter for a while and watched the swaggering style of the Cordoban maidens.

It was well into June, when on one of those Sundays while walking arm in arm with her sister and inventing a thousand stories, she ran into a man who looked familiar. Suddenly, the blush on her cheeks spread to her ears and she felt a great warmth in her body when she realized it was Juan del Rio.

"Good morning, Miss Angela and companions, good to see you," he said while thinking to himself, "My prayers have come true, thank you, my God!"

"Good morning to you, Juan. What a surprise to see you."

"But the surprise is mine, for I thought I would never again see you again."

"How did your studies go? Are you a doctor yet?"

"No, Angela. I still have one course left, but soon I will be. You won't need any help from me though, will you? Because with your sister and brother-in-law's permission, I can tell you that you look much prettier and healthier than when I saw you on the train."

"Juan, don't be over familiar; neither my wife nor I are in a position to allow the courtship of our Angela!"

"Excuse me, I didn't mean to be rude or overstep my bounds, but you will agree with me that Angela looked worse that day. Let me treat you to a lemonade, it's warm and I know a place where we can talk about your stay in Cordoba and its vicissitudes."

And that was how the university student, Juan del Río, began to draw closer to Angela. From time to time, he would go to see her, always in Severiana's presence, keeping his distance because of what he might profess. One night in October, while at the La Serena estate, Juan asked Antonio for permission to take a short walk alone with Angela. And this was granted.

"Angela, I want you to know what my intentions are. This year I will finish my studies and I will begin working as a doctor. And I firmly hope that you will be the one to accompany me on this journey as my fiancée. Now I do not have a large income, because it is my aunt in Seville, Dolores del Rio, who supports me, but I am sure and, I know for sure, that when my aunt meets you, she will understand the cause of my sleepless nights, which is none other than you. You are beautiful, your eyes shine with that light."

"Shush, Juan, you're making me jittery. I didn't imagine that your friendship would lead to feelings for me. It's one thing to come to the house to eat and to maintain a nice friendship with my brother-in-law, but it's quite another to woo me."

"Angela, you captivated my heart from the moment I saw how your brothers said goodbye to you, with the tenderness with which they embraced you and with the fear with which you remained on the train for four hours. I would have liked to have approached you and protected you, to have helped you to remove what was hurting you so much in your heart and to remove the pain from your eyes. But I could not overcome my shyness until the end of the journey, when I found the perfect excuse to address you without being taken for an opportunist."

"Juan, whenever you have addressed me, you have always done so with respect and politeness. I beg you not to court me. I...."

"I know, Angela. Antonio told me everything that happened. I've known about your misfortune for months. That's why I let time pass until I saw your smile."

"I did not know that you were aware of my misfortune. Now I feel ashamed and embarrassed, for nothing more ever happened between Samuel and me than a brief courtship."

"I have never doubted you, Angela, nor your honor nor your worth. Tell me, do you think you are capable of falling in love with me?"

"I don't know, Juan. I can't, and I don't dare, ask you to wait any longer, because I don't deserve such a blessing."

"From the sound of your words, you haven't forgotten Samuel, and that's normal. I don't want an answer right now, but I did want you to know my intentions. I'm just going to go straight ahead and say it... I love you, Angela."

"Don't say that, Juan. Don't say that word that's cursed for me; don't repeat it, for God's sake. It makes my soul bleed. Excuse me, Juan, I have to go."

Juan del Rio had made a full-fledged declaration, but Angela would never be able to love him; it was impossible to fill the void of Samuel's love. And why couldn't she? Because when a person falls head over heels in love and it is snatched away without time to get used to the idea, that love is not torn out, it remains a thorn embedded deep inside and no matter how much it is treated, that hurt takes root and becomes entrenched.

And so, Angela felt her own anguish. Her love did not disappear, rather it was mitigated until it created the illusion of its death, but to love another person was a bigger promise. It was to feel much more, in those moments when she realized that the thought of brushing her hand against Juan's or a stolen kiss made her feel bad, uncomfortable, dirty, as if she was killing the memory of Samuel. But hadn't Samuel forgotten about her? In her brothers' last letters, they had told her that he had been courting Miss Adela since the May holidays, which had hurt her tremendously. Nevertheless, she was not capable of allowing herself to be courted by Juan. She was still faithful to her feelings.

Angela's life centered on her work and her desire to learn to read and write. She had very little time left to practice, but she tried every night by candlelight. She worked as a maid in a well-to-do house in the city of Cordoba. The couple had two tremendously beautiful daughters, but at the same time, they were very surly with their parents and anyone else who got close to them, but Angela, with her stories and legends, drew them to her. Little by little her presence became an addictive routine, since not only did the girls listen to her stories, but also the rest of the servants and the lady of the house.

One evening, it was Christmas Eve, the lady sent for her and Angela came quickly to her. When she entered the great hall, Doña Agueda, who was gathered with her friends from the Adoration of the Blessed Sacrament group, entreated her to sit next to them. Angela, embarrassed, declined the offer and stood a little away from the group, leaning against the wooden sideboard.

Once the last of the Adorers who had arrived at the house had stopped chattering, Doña Agueda introduced them at length to her employee, but this time not as a "maid or servant", but as a person close to the family, whose gift of storytelling had made her very special to her and to the girls.

Angela expected the lady to demand a story, but she didn't because they were there to meet her and prove to the parish priest that Angela was sufficiently educated to be baptized and receive communion. And so it was that all those ladies of position came to love and appreciate her in such a way that, little by little, hey made her a lady of admiration worthy of admiration, teaching her not only religion, but also manners, phrases, gestures, hairstyles, and some pastimes and special recipes.

After a few months, Angela was a full-fledged woman, beautiful, sweet and full of humanity and tenderness. This was the opinion of Juan del Rio and some other neighbors who were already hopelessly in love with her. However, Angela's life was engulfed in learning, with knowing how to be and in the faith that came from knowing more about herself.

Spring will soon come. Almost a year in Cordoba. It seemed that everything had been a dream or one of those nightmares, which, though they begin with sadness, their ending, even if it is not the most beautiful, does have the flavor of conquering oneself. But whatever it was, she had overcome the feeling of being a rag that nobody wanted, someone who had no future because she is nothing.

"Mrs. Severiana Blanco?"

"Yes, that's me."

"An urgent telegram for you."

"My God, it can't be."

It was the worst news possible for the two sisters: The shoemaker had died. The night before there had been an unlucky accident. As he was leaving his workshop, a horse-drawn cart had run him over and the village doctor could do nothing for him.

The two sisters were devastated, neither was able to say or do anything but stare into each other's eyes. They no longer had the pillar that sustained them, that man weak in constitution, but so great inside; that man who was so poverty-stricken yet with an abundant stock of thoughts; that man incapable of bringing great sustenance to their home, yet who had taught them the most valuable riches: to know and understand that "his daughters were as free and equal as his sons"; that they had the independence and freedom to choose their own path, just as being different from the rest of their world, which considered mediocrity a virtue, was not a blight but dignity.

That man was dead. What were they to do? They had to go back to Bellavista de la Jara.

Angela had never once considered returning. Her life was apparently in Cordoba. There she was happy, protected and safe. She felt that she could become a young lady because there, no one would accuse her of being the shoemaker's daughter.

And now the shoemaker was gone. She could no longer show off her cooking, her ladylike gestures, her awkward way of reading aloud and the scribbling she did when she wrote.

"Severiana, I am afraid."

"Of what, Angela?"

"Of getting to the village, seeing my father's corpse, seeing the people, whatever they say about me, they all know that I left to forget Samuel and that he forgot me, because they didn't want me in his house because of whose daughter I am."

"You're afraid to see him, aren't you?"

"Yes, Severiana, I can't even imagine what damned chance I will have."

The sisters arrived in Bellavista de la Jara at sunset that May afternoon. The sunset, a fiery orange tone, lit up the three mountains, which resembled three great burning tongues, reflecting the heat that was rising throughout Angela's body. The heat was even more noticeable when they got out of Don Anastasio's truck, with whom they managed to hitch a ride from Andújar.

They stopped in the Plaza. There the villagers, sitting on the benches, chewed the fat, but all their talk was about the shoemaker's unfortunate accident. When they saw them get out of the hauler's truck in scrupulous mourning, all eyes were fixed on them, especially on Angela, who had really changed. That little girl of sixteen was now quite a young lady, elegant in her walk and gestures, and, most surprisingly, the way she moved with such charisma. Her high heels and black stockings gave style to her legs; the narrow black skirt hinted at a slim but curvy body; her white blouse that, with the incipient breeze of the evening, stuck to her torso; all combined to proclaim her emblematic of womanhood. More than a few wanted to give her their condolences, something that in other times they would not have ever considered, but now her serene beauty was a magnet with an attraction stronger than gravity itself.

The apothecary's son did not hesitate; he approached the women and asked them to escort them to the house, but Severiana replied with a dry, "thank you, but I'm sure we remember the way. Besides, we need to stretch our legs, which are numb from the trip", and the sisters slowly left to make their way home, their childhood home, grieving for their dead father.

When they arrived at the dwelling, the smell of humanity, of a whole town feeling his death, tiredness from a whole night of tears, was a biting sensation. Almost without perceiving that lacerating sensation, their siblings rushed out like a hurricane to embrace them. The union between them touched everyone present. The mourners did not have to fake tears because they flowed effortlessly from their eyes. Emotion and grief folded back their fears. She was now safe in the arms of her older brothers.

The burial was to take place first thing in the morning. The night was long for everyone; the encounter with the dead father, whose rupture with life was instant, was serene, without wails or exaggerated gestures that would have made the moment comical.

They prayed at the foot of the coffin, wept in silence and intuited the same thoughts to recite the dawn rosary and requiem.

Although their father was an atheist and freethinker, the strong faith ingrained in the daughters left no doubt that his burial would be religious. This was also the wish of the village priest himself, the shoemaker's closest friend.

Angela got up early. She kneaded a good amount of dough and went to the oven. There she vented her sorrow by digging her fingers into the dough and banging it again and again against the table. Once again relentless tears streamed down her face and dropped into her hands. She made seven loaves, one for each sibling, and with the leftover dough, some bread rolls for the children of Maria, the shepherdess, who saw food everywhere but on their little tin plates. She shook off her apron, folded it daintily with the peace that comes from work well done, and weeping with grief, put the loaves in the basket, tied up her hair and, bidding farewell to everyone, prepared to leave.

As she met with her fellow countrywomen, it was all hugs and heartfelt words, but also pushes and shakes that made her loosen the bun she had tied in the morning, which left her long wavy hair in the wind of Bellavista. With her pitiful little face, her dark wavy hair loose from so much shaking, her basket of bread and her apron over her shoulder, she walked crestfallen without looking up from the ground. And then she was at the square. Her legs seemed to weigh two hundredweight. It was very hot, so she decided to stop at the fountain and wash her face. The cool, clear water made her feel light and relieved as she washed away the kisses and drool of so many women eager to offer their condolences.

"Angela, good morning. How are you feeling?"

"Samuel! I didn't expect to see you here," she said, wiping her still wet lips on her apron with her hands, unable to raise her eyes to look at him and with her heart in her mouth.

"Once again at the same fountain, my dear Angela, in the same place where I saw you a year or so ago."

"That's right, Samuel," she confirmed, stepping back. "I hope your family is well."

"Yes, Angela, they are. But how are you? I am very sorry to hear about the death of your dear father. Such an unfortunate accident."

"We are all sorry. It has been a great loss. My siblings and I still needed his care and presence."

"Angela, you look so different. But let me help you with the basket, you look tired. Although, I will also tell you that you look beautiful with those little drops of water on your cheeks."

"Samuel, don't look at me like that, I beg you. I'm all messed up, out of sorts, and my eyes are like burst tomatoes."

"Don't say such things. You are more beautiful than ever, and I can't stop looking at you, because I have your eyes in the depths of my soul."

"Don't go on, Samuel, I beg you," she implored with some anger, taking a step back.

"Angela, my heart is coming out of my shirt. Let me talk to you."

Looking sideways she began to speak:

"Samuel, it's been a year. You belong to someone else, Miss Adela. I have matured and I will not allow anyone to make me feel like dirt again, nor will I allow anyone to make me feel ashamed of my humble roots. I will never again allow anyone to tell me that I am not worthy because of who my father was. That I swear by my father, who I hope is in glory."

"Angela, look into my eyes, don't you see anything in them? Let me tell you: I love you with all my being, there's no more love inside me for anyone else. I haven't stopped missing you for a single night or day, remembering your hands, the smell of your skin, feeling the wetness of your tears. Either we get married or I'll continue to die little by little every day, because love doesn't kill quickly, it does it by a thousand cuts that annul the joy of living; the only dream I have is to live at your side. I don't care about estates, inheritances, antiquated beliefs, my father and my family, my life, you are mine as I am yours! There is no Samuel without Angela and vice versa. Don't you see that I can't live without you? Can't you see that it tears my soul apart not to have you? Can't you see that you are my everything? What do I have to do to make you believe in me once and for all?"

"Samuel, I... I want to be yours!"

"From this moment on, you are my dearest Angela forever and ever."

Chapter IV
The First Letters

Samuel, with tears in his eyes and his heart galloping like a thoroughbred, took Angela by the waist and without giving her any warning, he wrapped her around his body and kissed her slowly, feeling for the first time the taste of his beloved's lips. He slowly separated himself from her without ceasing to admire her, kissed her hands with infinite tenderness, took the basket and prepared to accompany her home. But then, dropping a bombshell, he changed direction without warning, and grabbing her hand, he pulled her to the casino.

It was the first time that Angela had entered the casino, a place forbidden to women, not by statutes or membership regulations, but because no one would welcome a woman's intrusion in the men's place of leisure. It was their little sanctuary; where sometimes the cards became daggers; where the vice of gambling was of such magnitude that they gambled everything except for their woman, and who knows, maybe even that too. So, it is quite understandable that a woman's toe had never stepped over the threshold of the aforementioned place.

However, Samuel wanted to break the rules, every barrier created by male supremacy. He wanted to do it, he needed to do it, not for himself alone, but to make his Angela stand up to anyone who wanted to question the greatness of her being. It is natural that he wanted to stand up for himself since the notable day that his father had, in front of all those present, threatened to disinherit him if he married "the shoemaker's daughter", because there were some who were in favor of the estrangement and also others who considered him a brave man. He also did it for his family, the Almena family, who had never married outside of their social circle. He wanted, in front of everyone, to ensure that his father and grandfather knew of his decision, whatever happened.

Angela slowed down at the main entrance, cringing. She did not feel prepared to face Don Armando's rudeness. However, Samuel brushed the lock of hair out of her face, kissed her forehead and said in her ear,

"Angela, nobody will treat you badly in front of me; no one ever again, as long as I live! Now, look me in the face and don't ever lower your chin again. We will go in together and everyone will respect you, including my father and grandfather."

"Samuel, I feel like shouting our love to the four winds, but to go in there, to see how they pierce me with their eyes and seek your father's approval… I am already overwhelmed. I feel so many things that my head is going to explode; I can't take it all in."

"Come on, calm down. I'll do the talking."

Samuel decisively opened the door to let Angela in. The silence was sepulchral. Then everyone rose from their seats, including Don Armando and Don Emilio. She raised her chin, took a deep breath and said,

"Good morning, gentlemen."

Everyone responded in one way or another, some with a hand gesture, others with a nod of the head, others with a word of greeting. But the most special greeting was from Don Armando Almena.

"Good morning, Angela, I am very sorry for the loss of your father. I can't imagine the pain you must be feeling not having been able to say goodbye to him. The worst thing is that I feel guilty about it."

"Don Armando, please don't blame yourself for God's crooked ways."

"Father," Samuel interjected, "as you can see...."

"Shut up, Samuel. I haven't finished talking to Angela yet. This is no place for a young lady like you to be in, but since the caprice of destiny has chosen it to be here, well, this will be the place where I apologize to you. I beg your pardon for my pride. And, in front of everyone, because that is how it is, that is how it should be, I beg you to accept my son as your fiancé. And there's an end to it."

"Father, Angela is already 'my dearest Angela'."

"Daughter, give me a hug and forgive us."

So, Don Armando approached her, excited and wanting to hug her. He was overcome with emotion, but also with the hope of finally making his son smile again.

But no one noticed that Miss Adela's father was also present in the casino with his blood running wild. It was the mayor who grabbed him by the arm and in a low voice said to him,

"You know he hasn't even missed your daughter since he left your house months ago. They haven't seen each other for a long time, so stop looking for a cape to fight that bull, because no one will cheer for you, not even from afar."

The following days felt like minutes. Such was the happiness of both that they thought they were living in a dream, but the dream had a dark guest: it was time to part again. Samuel was at the age of obligatory military service. To be separated from his beloved Angela burned him inside, but his duty was clear. It was for this reason that Don Armando used his influence so that, just as family money had fixed it for him, so it would for his son also.

Don Armando Almena, according to the military service record that he showed Samuel, had spent twelve years in the military! But in fact, it was false, because, thanks to a generous boodle, he was spared from any assignment and was discharged after a short period, even though his record showed a full twelve years. Don Armando decided to fight for his son to be spared, as he had been, but it proved impossible. However, money still had some effect and strings were pulled and recommendations made, wonderful recommendations, which led to Samuel entering the army in the Húsares de la Princesa, a cavalry regiment.

"Samuel, you are going to have to do your military service, but not just like everyone else."

"Tell me, father."

"You are going to serve in the Húsares de la Princesa, a regiment based in Madrid. Entry is solely by recommendation, and you know that we Almena have ways of opening doors, many times without having to owe too many favors, which could later come to light. Listen to me, I'll tell you a little about it.

"The Hussars were formed in Spain in June 1705, they were initially called "the Hussars of Death", you can't even imagine the courage and daring they showed, even death feared them. But they were few and they were like the Guadiana, entering and leaving the military panorama. Take note, Samuel, in March 1833, the Hussars Regiment of Princess Maria Isabel Luisa, daughter of Ferdinand VII and heir to the throne, Isabella II, was finally created.

"They were created with the intention of having an elegant parade troop, in the style of the English regiments, as an escort of honor for the Princess, and this is indicated by the fact that the

Queen Mother Maria Christina, herself chose her favorite color, light blue for their uniforms."

"Father, are you sending me to a place for young ladies or do I have to go to ballet classes to get out of doing military service?"

"Don't be silly. It's unbelievable that you don't know your own father. Now, shut up and listen. You may think that their origin was frivolous, but they were quickly deployed in battle, and for that reason, just three years later, for their heroic behavior in the taking of Orduña, in 1836, and other successes that they won in following years, they obtained their first Ribbon of the Royal and Military Order of San Fernando for their standard.

"But as always, the vicissitudes of the politics of this country determined its dissolution at the end of the Carlist wars. But as there were vested interests, after its dissolution, the Húsares de la Princesa appeared again in 1855, thus testifying once again their bravery by fighting in the front line in the war of Africa in 1860.

"In short, to make it clear to you, the recommendation you carry is fine gold, you are going to belong to one of the greatest regiments in Spain. It goes without saying that an Almena lives up to his surname in everything he undertakes, and now you can go remembering it as you leave."

Another farewell. Once again it was time for distance to separate their love, their desire to get married, to touch each other for the first time, to be joined without beginning or end, but the military was waiting for him, and there was no turning back.

"Angela, look at me, everything will pass soon. Besides, Madrid is very fine. I'm sure it will be interesting, otherwise I promise to write you every day, but on the condition that I receive a letter from you in reply, don't be lazy with the pen, I need to feel you close."

"You won't forget me, Samuel, will you? Ladies abound in Madrid, they are elegant and pretty, and your eyes peal like bells when you see a beautiful young lass."

"For me the only beautiful woman is you, and what's more, I promise not to look to the left or to the right, only to the front, so as not to bump into one." He smiled mischievously, his face all innocent, to ease the farewell.

"Samuel, it's taken us so long to get here! We've left so many troubles behind us! I feel vexed, uneasy, with doubts about...."

"We? Look, Angela, don't say such nonsense again, it's just a 'see you soon', they'll give me leave and I'll come running like crazy to steal a kiss from you, and I hope that on that occasion I can have the joy of you letting me give you many more, that you put your arms around me every time you can. Come on, my beautiful rose, I'll take your smell and your little smile with me! Can't you see I'm dying of the sorrow parting, of having to leave you! I love you, my dear Angela."

Samuel left like all the recruits by train, with his lunch in his bundle and with the dream of returning soon; but he also carried with him the fear of the unknown and the uncertainty of arriving in a city as colossal as Madrid, accustomed as he was to the small-town life of Bellavista de la Jara.

Madrid, July 6, 1930.

Dear Angela, I received your letter, and from what I read you are feeling a bit delicate, which I am very sorry for. I remain without news of any posting.

Regarding what you tell me about your sister Severiana's invitation to go to the bullfights and not being able to do so because you are sick, I am very sorry. I hope you are recovered now and with my blessing you can go to the next one; do not forget to give my regards to your dear sister.

I went to the hospital last Monday to visit Gregoria, but my surprise was that she had gone home last month because she was feeling better.

As for your comment regarding my father's arrival, I don't know anything, since I haven't received a letter from him for more than two weeks. The truth is that I am very much looking forward to his arrival, because I miss him and because I am short of funds. To my misfortune I have lost twenty-five pesetas that they sent me the other day. I kept them in the purse that I put in the left pocket of my pants. Anyway, I went for a walk and I went into a store to buy some socks and a tie, but when I went to pay, I found that instead of the purse there was a hole the size of a potato. Imagine the deal I could have made, but now all I can say is that I am left without a peseta. And everyone at home asks for more money, so I beg you not to say anything at all.

I'm homesick, but I have been told that maybe soon they will grant me leave; please, don't say anything to my father or grandfather about my leave. Who knows, any day now, when you open the door, I'll steal from you one of those hidden kisses that drive me crazy but which you never give me.

Without further ado I send my regards to all your brothers and sisters, and you receive the affection of the one who loves you and yearns to see you very soon.

Samuel Almena

In this simple way, his life in Madrid and the exchange of epistles began. Samuel used to write during his break, sitting at a cold table in whichever café in Madrid, narrating his adventures and misadventures, his anecdotes and desires, closing his eyes or staring into the distance while he drew Angela's face, her voice, her hands in his mind. In those magical moments in which he would write, stopping time, to resurface in that other moment when she would read his missive.

I must admit that the Almenas were a bit absent-minded and that losing things was their specialty, but it was always futile destiny that played tricks on them with its little imps.

Madrid, July 22, 1930.

Dear Angela, I received your letter and am immensely joyful that you are well, as are all your family. I remain without news of my posting.

When I visited Norberto, I asked him to tell you what I do here, which in truth is very little. If the corporal doesn't give us orders, the sergeant does, but not very often. We leave the barracks when we want, as civilians, and we return at the time they tell us to. I will have my photograph taken when my finances improve so you can see how thin I am; but I will recover.

I'm getting to know Madrid. I wish you were here, because then I wouldn't go alone to the festivals, nor to the theater, nor to the operetta. So here I wait for you, because they neither give me leave nor do they give me a posting. They told me that maybe I can go for the Assumption of the Virgin in August, but also that if I take leave I can lose my posting, that doesn't suit me for anything in the world! Although you must know that I have an immense desire to go and see you, more than you can imagine, but patience, my little flower, I will come to you sometime.

When I finish writing I'm going to get ready, because I'm going with Marcial to the San Ginés chocolate shop, which is very crowded, not only for the chocolate and churros, but also because they say that the poets and writers who are there every afternoon are very important. It is true that the gatherings that they host leave everyone spellbound, and I, more than anyone, am left dumbfounded and feeling like an idiot who knows nothing. Afterwards, we're going to the theater to see an operetta. Since we don't have a cent at the end of the month, and you know I'm not going to ask my father for more as if he were a vending machine, we have discovered that if you go as part of the claque you get in for free or very cheap and you clap or whistle when they tell you. Sometimes I'm so excited listening to those voices that my coworkers have to nudge me to do what they tell us to do.

Angela, I'll say goodbye for now. Give my regards to your brothers and sisters, and you receive the affection of the one who loves you and yearns to see you soon.

Samuel Almena

Samuel was excited, he was not aware of the historical and literary moment in which he was living as he snacked on coffee with churros and observed the bohemian-looking people, scholars of letters and other arts that surrounded him. He wondered who they were when he wrote to his *Angela* from the Callejón de San Gines; he did not know that the man on the right was Ramón María Valle Inclán, who every day at the same time sat at the same table, or so he said of himself in Luces de Bohemia, which was published in 1920.

Samuel little by little was talking with the habitués of the café, he liked to remain silent listening to what was said about the ins and outs of the Republic, the state of the monarchy, the most hidden secrets of his thoughts, and Samuel, a gatecrasher, dumbfounded and excited, feeling provincial and perhaps not understanding many of the things that happened there, remained like a statue. He was being enlightened every moment, without realizing it, about history, literature, theater and zarzuela.

Madrid, August 12, 1930.

Dear Angela, I have just received your letter, which has helped me to feel a great joy to see that you are well as are all your family, I remain without news of a posting.

You tell me to write when I'm coming, but it's impossible to find out. Until the commanding officer arrives and informs me of my posting, I can't move. And you can't imagine how fed up I am with Madrid and how much I want to come home to see you, to eat a butter cake or some hare stew.

You also tell me that your sister Severiana is going to go to the August fair. I hope she enjoys going to the bullfights; I think this year they'll be fighting our own.

Angela, try to find out what is going on with my family. It has been twenty-four days since I last received a letter and I have written them twice now. Their silence worries me. Please pass by my house and ask the maid how they are, but be careful as she's a terrible gossip; we don't want our affairs all-round the town. Whatever she tells you, let me know immediately, because I do not know what's caused this delay. I hope that my grandfather and father are well, that the pasture is being well managed and that the bulls are not fighting each other. I need to know, dearest Angela.

Without anything else to say, give my regards to your brothers, sisters and brothers-in-law, and you receive the affection of the one who loves you and yearns to see you very soon.

Samuel Almena

The long-awaited August holidays arrived, no one showed up at Angela's door, and sorrow filled her soul. Disillusioned, and knowing that Samuel frequented theaters and cafés, she imagined a thousand and one possibilities of being forgotten. But when her sorrows pierced her heart, she closed her eyes and saw his blue eyes penetrating her soul, then she let herself be carried away on daydreams and memories: their rides to the threshing floor and through the pasture; his hand clasping hers and that touching way of his to brush the lock of hair from her cheek.

She spent her time helping with the housework, reading a lot, as well as telling her fabulous legends and tales that her neighbors and friends loved so much. Storytelling was the gift that always accompanied her; inventing stories with characters that eager listeners requested, and making the world succumb to those big green eyes that sometimes seemed to have a life of their own.

Madrid, October 6, 1930.

His Excellency, the Count of Torrecilla de Cameros.

Dear Genaro:

With reference to your kind letter dated July 2, last, in which you appealed to me to favor the soldier, Samuel Almena Perez, of the 19th Cavalry Regiment, the Húsares de la Princesa, I send you the letter that I received from the Colonel of the said Corps upon his return to Court, and I send it to you, signifying that, in thanking him, I have reiterated my determination that your protege be granted a posting.

Many best wishes to your family and a big hug from your cousin, who loves you.

Gabriel

Such was the degree of friendship between Don Armando and Don Genaro Alonso Castrillo, Count of Torrecilla de Cameros, that not only did Samuel join the Húsares de la Princesa with a recommendation, but, abundantly better, he obtained an even more comfortable posting as a civilian, and outside the barracks, which allowed Samuel to do his military service like a king. And as favor is repaid with favor, the Colonel was well rewarded with closed-door bullfights in the Almena's pasture. Once his son's new posting was confirmed, Don Armando invited his dear friend Genaro, who appeared with his entourage of friends, among them the master bullfighter, Marcial Lalanda, and there, in Bellavista de la Jara for the Pilar festivities, they could delight in his art, and in particular with the pass that made him famous, the "lance de mariposa" (butterfly dodge).

Madrid, October 11, 1930.

His Excellency the Count of Torrecilla de Cameros.

Dear Genaro:

I am pleased to send you the attached letter I have received from the Colonel of the Regiment of Húsares de la Princesa, by which you will see that your protégé, Samuel Almena Perez has been granted a posting outside the barracks as he wished.

Much is celebrated by your cousin who hugs you.

Gabriel

Chapter V
Returning To My
Small Hometown

Samuel reported back to his superiors, and with the free time he had, every day he strolled through the Madrid that fascinated him so much. One such day he boarded the first section of the Sol-Cuatro Caminos metropolitan railroad. There, at Sol, he began to stroll slowly, savoring each step, looking at the palaces of the bourgeoisie and nobility, who sought royal favor, which were located in the vicinity of the Royal Palace, the Plaza Mayor and the Plaza de España. Almost without realizing it, he entered one of them, and when he was stopped by one of the employees, they began to chat, coming to the conclusion that they were almost fellow countrymen. So, just as if it were in a story, Samuel went inside, he was surrounded by luxurious rooms and furniture. He gawked at the arrival of a horse-drawn carriage that reached the double staircase so that the gentlemen would not have to leave the building when they got into their carriage; the pond lined with beautiful camellias; statues and Romanesque capitals scattered throughout the garden; and the library, with the furniture smelling of ancient knowledge and Carlist strategies.

He left the palace to go to the ballroom. While the servants talked around him, like a gatecrasher, he imagined his Angela corseted, with the tight waist of the Indian silk dress, making delicate gestures with her fan, waiting for the Count of Torrecilla de Cameros to ask her to dance.

In this reverie, he set off for the Palace of the Orient, where at midday sharp, *voilà*, there was the "march of the Royal Guard", led by the cavalry units, followed by the artillery pieces and finally, the sentries on foot.

He felt so at ease daydreaming, enraptured, abstracted and transported to past stories of honor and homeland, but he was getting hungry and cold. So, without thinking twice he set out for the chocolate shop in San Ginés, the one that he visited so often. But he did not really feel like chocolate; and he remembered the Lhardy and went there to have a delicious hot broth with a splash of sherry that delighted his taste buds and accentuated his appetite. When he arrived at the barracks, he found he had been sent for.

"Samuel Almena, report to your colonel." So, Samuel was called in by the colonel, who appreciated him so much and did so much to get him a good assignment.

"Yes, sir."

"Samuel, I am proud to have known you, you enlisted as an Andalusian gentleman with airs and graces, and now I return you to your father as a man of culture and refined tastes, with well learned trades and being honorable. And let me remind you what happened in Spain: the revolutionary committee assumed power on the 14th of April last year and when the Republic was proclaimed in the Casa de Correos of the Puerta del Sol; remember how wild the crowd went? They are going to dissolve us, Samuel. The republican-socialist conjunction that won against the monarchists, in the April 12 elections. That has meant the disintegration of the monarchy and the advent of the Second Republic. Therefore, I am handing you your license, so that you can leave as soon as possible to return to your hometown and to the arms of the lass you love so much. Give my sincerest greetings to your father, Don Armando Almena. Now, do you need money for your journey?"

"My colonel, it has been a great pleasure to serve in your 19th Cavalry Regiment, the Húsares de la Princesa, and an honor to be under your command. There had been some talk of disbanding, but nothing definite. I feel somewhat downcast and abandoned, as if somehow, we too are a decayed monarchy. But they are only vain thoughts compared to the joy of returning to my hometown, where my fiancée is tired of embroidering trousseaus and longs to see me. Thank you for everything, Colonel. I don't need any money to return home. And before I say goodbye, in Bellavista de la Jara, you and your family have not only my father's house, but also the pasture, if someday you feel like trying your luck with a calf or a cow.

"Here you are, Samuel, your license, and give me your hand, because life is very short and we don't know where we will see each other or if we will ever see each other again."

"With your permission, Colonel."

Samuel returned to Bellavista de la Jara, first by train to Vilches and from there in a truck belonging to a fellow provincial. The farewell to Madrid was bittersweet, because every step he took to Atocha became a beautiful memory of the days spent in the regiment with his great friends, taking care of the horses, training them and even going hungry due to the rations they were given during the first months. Later, in the offices and with a civilian pass, being, or rather considering himself a Madrilenian by adoption, he smiled thinking about what face grandfather Emilio would make when he told him about such adventures; the loss of the twenty-five pesos because of the hole in his pants; the letters that he missed so much and his happiness when he received them; the get-togethers over hot chocolates; with thousands and thousands of memories that made Madrid, for him, no longer a distant metropolis, but the home that took him in to make him a man.

As nobody knew he was arriving that night, Don Armando's house was locked up tight; the cats did not show off their jealousy and springtime infatuation; the silence transmitted the rhythm of the soles of his shoes. Accustomed to setting a firm pace, the carotid artery in his neck seemed to beat stronger than his own heart. "I'm home!" he thought.

He gripped the knocker tightly, the large bronze hand holding the ball made him feel cold, and without thinking he gave two raps.

"Who is it?

"Ah, there is someone home!"

"What time is this to wake good people up? Some lazy, debauched drunkard asking for a loaf of bread!" said Ramona, the maid, grumpily.

"It's me, Samuel" he called back.

"Oh, Master Samuel, may heaven and all its saints be praised for having appeared to me out of glory. If it isn't you, yourself! Come in, come in, come in, I'll prepare you some good food, God knows how long it's been since you've had something decent to eat! But when did you get here?"

"Well, Ramona, certainly the time from the garden to my father's house," he said, laughing out loud.

"What's the matter, Ramona? What's all this noise? My son! Father, Father, Father, Samuel has returned home!"

That night, April 20, 1931, became a Christmas Eve, wine, pork and grilled bacon. Ramona industriously cooked everything that the master liked: pickled partridge, mixed meat stew, porridge with toast, rice pudding; for a moment he thought he was a " San Anton pig", one of those that must be sacrificed after fattening him well.

He slept soundly until after sunrise when the bells of the clock in the Plaza reminded him that he was in his bed, in his house, in his hometown and close to his Angela. He jumped out of bed, called the servants and asked them to run him a bath, to take out his charcoal suit, white shirt and one of the collars he had brought from Madrid, to clean his black shoes thoroughly, to polish his watch and brush his black wide-brimmed hat.

He had his breakfast: muffins with oil, delicious freshly brewed coffee and half a butter cake. He tied up his hair, put on his hat and winked at the serving girls who, naturally, adored him.

"Good morning to you, ladies."

"Samuel!" Angela was petrified, as if she were a statue of salt at the sight of him. "What are you doing here?"

"Angela, my darling, only you could manage to say such a thing to me." He held back from kissing her on that mouth he adored so much, because her brothers and sisters were watching the encounter and he didn't want to embarrass her when their faces were less than a breath away. And as if the air should not touch her, Samuel cradled her in his arms and body as if there was nothing more in life."

Like any couple, following a decent time of courtship and having the possibility of being able to marry, Samuel and Angela were married on September 17, 1933.

In those days, weddings were not celebrated, but the wedding of the son of Don Armando and the daughter of the shoemaker was a big event in the whole county; not only the closest relatives of the happy couple attended, but also the good and the great of Bellavista de la Jara society, the best of the servants and the common class gathered that day.

The beautiful patio of the Almena's house was decorated with pots of geraniums, with garlands of roses, the floor was carpeted with rosemary from the Sierra Morena, and the smell of fields and pastures made the guests feel calm and at peace.

The meal was full of typical local dishes, so there was no shortage of pheasant and pickled partridge, chicken in egg and almond sauce, garlic pig, cod with onions, lamb or suckling pig, all washed down with wine that flowed lavishly through the glasses, as well as loaves of bread freshly baked by Uncle Pedro, Angela's relative. And as for dessert, homemade sweets with the scent of lemon and pineapple, such as wine donuts, ice creams, and the wedding cake made with sponge cake that was tipsy with brandy.

The lovers' faces did not cease to amaze those present, and it was rumored, even aroused some jealousy and envy among the guests, but nothing could darken such a happy moment. Even Miss Adela and her parents attended the wedding, now without rancor, having understood that love freely chooses the heart in which it wants to settle.

All the cheers for the bride and groom, some paso dobles, the usual songs, fandangos and plenty of guitar playing.

As the day went by, the mouths were satiated and the alcohol took its effect, groups began to become more intimate and smaller, until Angela sat down with the children of the gypsy Jimena and began to tell them the story of *La encantada del puerto (The Enchanted Lady of the Pass). All* the youngsters, and even the adults, despite knowing the legend, were absorbed by her voice and the sweetness with which she narrated the tale.

She had such a gift that she did not need school or grades to take the audience to her world, that inner world full of fantasy and creativity.

"Hush! It's time to hear what happened to *La encantada del puerto.*

"Many, many years ago, Bellavista de la Jara was reconquered from the infidels; very close to this house lived a Moorish family, the father's name was Abu-Eben and he had two daughters, Zaida and Zoraida, both of exceptional beauty. Father and daughters belonged to the most modest class of the infidels; they survived by cultivating the fields. But Abu-Eben, although very poor, was very well-educated. My father, the shoemaker, told me that it was the Arabs who introduced the irrigation system to this country. In addition, he was a brave and faithful warrior, being the right-hand man of the Mohammedan chiefs in that period of Bellavista's history.

"Abu-Eben tirelessly carried provisions of food and weapons to the castle, as well as the valuables and jewels that the inhabitants of Bellavista de la Jara possessed.

"That day he had left his daughters secluded in their modest and miserable dwelling. The two young women, calm, confidently awaited the realization of Allah's designs, but something could be felt in the air.

"At midday and to the sound of trumpets, kettledrums and voices of command, Bellavista was invaded by a multitude of horsemen who the Moorish army could not contain, while the remaining forces of the infidels were making themselves secure in the castle, but by carelessness or overconfidence, all had not taken their women and children.

"Zaida and Zoraida were at home when the alarm was raised,

"What's that noise" Zoraida asked her sister in alarm.

"I don't know. Perhaps brother warriors coming to our defense."

"But what if they are Christians? I don't want to think about it. What would become of us?"

"Well, I'm going to take a look," said Zaida boldly.

"Never!" interrupted Zoraida. "No way; obey the orders father gave us when he left. We have to make the house look like it's not inhabited and to hide ourselves as best we can."

"But, giving in to her curiosity, and without her sister Zoraida being able to prevent it, Zaida rushed to one of the small windows that gave light to the dark and narrow room located on the first, and only floor, of the house. Looking out, beneath that sculptural head of hair, her black eyes were petrified at the sight of the banners of Castile and Leon with the crosses that crowned them, and the martial aspect of the troops of the king of the Christians, Ferdinand III. Zaida was transfixed; her sister pulled her forcefully from the window and both, without saying a word to each other, cry in an embrace over the misfortunes they foresee for themselves and their father, whom they doubt they will ever see again.

"The castle had been under siege for eight days; there was nothing to eat and the fighting was becoming unbearable in the fortress, though not for lack of courage on the part of the besieged. Zaida and Zoraida, who are the same age, having been born a few minutes apart, wept bitterly for their misfortune. They remained locked up in their house. There was no possible consolation for the beautiful daughters of Mohammed. Some days had passed since the entry of the Christian troops, who did not yet possess the castle. One night, however, while Zaida and Zoraida were embracing and dumb with terror, they were suddenly surprised to hear the metallic sound of a key rattling in the lock. Both ran to the small door, agile as fawns responding to the barking of a dog, guessing who the visitor would be, and coming face to face with their father, haggard, panting and laden down with a bulky bundle on his back.

"Abu-Eben abruptly refused the affection they wanted to give him, and, not stopping to give explanations, in an imperative tone gave them the orders,

"Without losing time," he said to them, "prepare to flee. I have succeeded in escaping, thanks to my agility, by fastening a rope to my waist and being lowered from the castle walls. But I fear I have been seen, and perhaps they will pursue me, so it is necessary to hurry. Believing that the surrender of our last refuge is imminent, all the besieged have entrusted me to save their wealth by hiding it in a safe place, in the orchard at the pass, where we will find the suitable location for such a hiding place, and perhaps we can then leave this place to join our own.

"Pale, emaciated, and hardly breathing, they listened to what their father said, not daring to reply. They kept silent and quickly gathered the meager subsistence they had left before following their father out through the same door that he had entered minutes before. Almost crawling, snaking, joining their bodies to the walls of the houses, in an attempt to avoid the feared encounter with the patrols that surrounded the besieged hill. With a sack full of coins and precious metals on his shoulders, Abu-Eben marched with difficulty in front of his daughters.

"The moon illuminated them at intervals until they stopped in the orchard. They united, crying, in a close embrace believing they were out of danger and the emotion that seized them; already calmer, Abu-Eben addressed his daughters in these or similar words,

"In the place where we are, dear daughters, about twenty steps away, there is a cave that is known only to me, having had the good fortune to find in the time when my work was to cultivate this beautiful orchard. I found it one hot night in June, when I didn't know whether I was dreaming or awake. I witnessed an extraordinary thing that I don't want to remember; I saw strange and attractive figures coming out of those rocks, who with their beckoning gestures seemed to be calling me. At the same time, music and certain inexplicable vibrations drew me to that place.

Rather than leaving, I let myself be carried away, and in fact, in the place that was the object of that special attraction, I found an opening half covered by a large stone that, as if it had been opened with a spell, left free the access to a cave which, until then, had been completely hidden. Suddenly, I heard strange sounds; of trumpets, of the baying of packs and out-of-tune cries, which soon passed, having then disappeared just as suddenly as they had appeared. I have often thought since then that they had to be a dream. I closed that natural door, I left, and now I'm going to take advantage of my secret to deposit the riches, whose guardianship has been entrusted to me, in that hidden place."

"Father," exclaimed Zaida, impressed, "you frighten us with your story."

"I was fearful too, in spite of my fortitude," replied Abu-Eben, "and you may be sure that but for the terrible circumstances in which we have found ourselves, I should never have come to these parts, at precisely the same hour when I discovered that cave.

"Allah is great and Muhammad his prophet; what is written will come to pass," said the beautiful Zoraida.

"Let us go, then. You can help me in my enterprise," added their father, "and tomorrow we shall see the sun rise in Úbeda, where the sons of the prophet have security for their persons and goods."

"And having said this, he took a few steps towards a large stone which, at a push of his hands, moved aside to reveal an opening that led into a dark cave. The young women, filled with more fear than astonishment, followed their father, and he, anxious to finish the mission that had been entrusted to him as soon as possible, entered the cave with the sack over his shoulder, followed by his daughters. He placed his precious load on a rock and, at that very moment, as if in an incantation, there suddenly sounded out of tune shouts, trumpet noises and the baying of a pack; Abu-Eben jumped in surprise, his daughters followed him, he wanted to hide the entrance of the cave and touched the stone of the access, with such haste, that it moved quickly, the entrance hole closed and prevented the exit of the beautiful Zoraida, who was last in line, and she was locked in with the treasure forever.

"The following day, or so the old men affirm, the castle of Bellavista having been taken, Mr. Benavides, its conqueror, sent patrols to the surrounding areas, and upon arriving at the pass, they found not far from the abundant spring that exists there, two human bodies horribly torn to pieces; it was only possible to say that one was that of a traditionally dressed Muslim, judging by the remains of his attire, and the other, that of a Moorish woman, from whose intact head the features of a singular and extraordinary beauty could still be admired.

That is the legend of the *Enchanted Lady of the pass*; this is how the old women tell it, swearing that the event took place in the month of June, on the night of the feast of St John, and that every year on that same night and at the same time, you will hear the sounds of bugles and trumpets, out of tune cries and the baying of packs. It is then that, through those twists and turns, a Moorish lady appears to walk; she is richly adorned with the treasures that Abu-Eben deposited in that place; and that according to tradition, she seems to be looking for her father and her lost sister."

Samuel looking at her, loving her every word, every little sigh that came out of the mouth of the one who was now his wife. Only one idea rumbled in his brain that, no matter how he felt in his body, from that day on, he could now steal all the kisses and caresses that he had imagined during their courtship. He felt she was his, entirely and eternally his. His body reacted to every thought as if it no longer belonged to him, as if he was only thinking about the moment of loving her.

"Angela, come," he whispered in her right ear.

"Yes." She looked up at him with the brightest eyes she could ever have and a shiver went down the back of her neck to her belly.

"It's time to say goodbye. Give a kiss to your brothers and sisters, while I go kiss my father and grandfather." He stared into her eyes with a passion that was more than evident.

The alcove was spacious, the sheets an immaculate white; the washbasin was prepared with white cotton towels embroidered with both their initials; thepants pressed perfectly positioned for Samuel's suit; and his bed facing the mirrors of the polychrome wooden closet. Angela entered very slowly, observing every detail, noticing the mirrors where her bridal-dressed figure was dimly reflected by the dim light of the silver candelabra on the dresser. She watched Samuel approach as she felt his hands on her shoulders. Delicately he removed the flower hairpins that gathered her hair, until the moment came when her long hair overflowed down her back. Then Samuel gathered her in his hands to kiss her and sniff her deeply, sinking into her neck and slowly kissing the skin that peeked through the neckline of her dress. Angela, petrified, absorbed in the caresses and not knowing what to do held still. While Samuel slowly undid the endless buttons of her dress, it seemed like eternal seconds; she didn't know what would come next, but she wished he would finish unbuttoning it so he could feel more and more of her. When she least expected it, her dress fell to the floor and she saw herself again in the mirror. Samuel blew out the candles exhaling softly, turned her slowly and their mouths merged in the most passionate kiss, taking her towards the bed, while their hands undressed their bodies. Then Samuel began to make love to her with the utmost tenderness, devouring with kisses every inch of her skin until he made her his, his, his.

Samuel was gently awakened by the ray of sunlight that warmed his face, he looked towards the window trying to remember where he was. In that instant between sleep and wakefulness, when he still remembered what he had dreamed, he was not able to understand what was stirring inside him. Then, a second later, he realized that the body sleeping next to him was that of his beloved Angela. He had the foolish impulse to wake her up with a kiss, but his avid hand remained suspended, tracing the curves of her body adorned by the white sheets. He lay back on the goose feather pillow, an aftertaste of peace and desire running through him. He was only able to admire her: her wavy black hair fanned out on the pillow; her eyes closed like an angel, living up to her name; her mouth, oh, her mouth! How many times he had longed for her and now she was his to kiss as many times as he wanted, to taste her in eternal kisses at night and with warm, hidden touches during the day.

"Good morning, Father," he said, clearing his throat.

"God keep you, son, how did you sleep?" he asked with a mischievous and laughing tone.

"So very well, thank you."

"And Angela? Maybe she's still sleeping."

"No, she is preening. She says she wants to go to the cemetery to visit her parents' graves and then I want to take her to the pasture. Do you mind father if we don't have lunch with you?"

"How could I mind? The married man wants a house and I want grandchildren."

"Father! If I got her pregnant the first time, it would be a miracle."

"Your mother, may God rest her soul, conceived you on our wedding night, so keep in mind that the greyhound's whelp comes from a purebred. Go on, have a cup of coffee, it will come in handy, and if you add a little brandy, it will taste even better."

Angela slowly appeared in the living room of the Bodegon house. The cadence of her steps, the sound of her heels and the sun that outlined her silhouette behind her, left those present captivated. Her hair was not completely tied back, only a silver hairpin on the left side, spilling her hair like a hairpin over her chest. Samuel and Don Armando, as gentlemen do, stood up, and Marcial pulled Angela's chair from the table so that she could take her seat. Suddenly, she felt all eyes on her and a heavy silence that made her uncomfortable.

"Good morning, Don Armando. Good morning, everyone."

"Good morning, Angela, I hope you had a good night's rest on your first night in this house."

"Yes, thank you, Don Armando. The truth is that the bedroom is like a palace, it lacks no detail."

"Daughter, I don't want you to call me Don Armando. If you want and if it doesn't offend you, I would be extremely happy if you treated me as a father. Yours is gone and now you live under my roof."

"It's hard for me to do, Don Armando, you have always been Don Armando," she concluded, smiling.

"Well, it's about time," said Grandpa Emilio, suddenly entering the living room, "Can I have a kiss, pretty lady?"

"Grandfather, don't be so forward with my wife," Samuel emphasized with possessiveness. "Maybe she doesn't feel like it."

"It's alright, Don Emilio. A kiss doesn't offend when it's genuinely given," she replied, getting up and bringing her mouth close to his cheek.

"You had a beautiful wedding, the whole town came, rich and poor, gypsies and gorgers, not even the precentor was absent," said Don Armando.

"Father, I never thought it was possible to be so happy or that so many people could fit in the courtyard and in the halls."

Impulsive and unpredictable as always, Ramona entered, singing a folk song, with a tray of food left over from the wedding, ham, bacon, tomatoes, olive oil and the ice creams that grandfather Emilio liked so much. She greeted everyone and looked at the bride and groom with a mischievous expression.

"What! All right?"

"Of course," said Angela, getting up to help Ramona.

"Oh, no, ma'am! I'll do everything now. You are no longer the shoemaker; you are Doña Angela."

"Don't you ever refer to your mistress as a shoemaker, Ramona," said Don Armando authoritatively.

"Don't worry, father," Angela said in a trembling voice, "I am not offended because I am, and always will be the shoemaker's daughter, even though I am now Samuel Almena's wife. My character has not changed, my simplicity will not be disturbed, and my position will be a combination of where I come from, where I live and what God wants me to be."

"Oh, my daughter! What lessons you give us with that tenderness and sweetness that characterizes you," said grandfather Emilio. "And you, Ramona, let's see if you can't be more subtle as it seems that you have the mouth of a toad."

"Can I offer anyone anything else or can I go as I'm clearly not welcome here?"

Angela was no longer a stranger, now they wanted to treat her as a daughter and, of course, as a wife. She felt strange and at the same time happy in her new fur dress.

Their horse rides through the pasture made her feel free, riding through the fields at a fast gallop, clinging to the waist of her Samuel, was a pleasure that seemed almost forbidden because of the delight it caused her. Losing herself among the oaks and the smell of rockrose, letting herself be loved by her husband, without being disturbed by anything or anyone. One couldn't be happier!

The love, the laughter, the passionate kisses, the madness of the newlyweds had filled the house of the Bodegon, but Angela began to feel unwell, she had not had any bleeding for two months, when on November 9, suddenly, a strong abdominal pain twisted her, and she collapsed and fell in the courtyard of the house. No one saw her, she wanted to scream, but she was unable to utter a moan, the pain paralyzed her. Marcial, who was coming out of the stables, found her in a pool of blood, he began to call for help and everyone came running in panic. Samuel jumped on his horse and rushed to the doctor, but when he returned home, the village midwife, who was a neighbor, had already helped poor Angela; she had lost her baby.

But after this episode, in the spring of 1934, she became pregnant again, the joy and care she received from her Samuel and the whole family led to the pregnancy having a happy ending, and it was then that on November 2, 1934, her firstborn, Manuel Almena Blanco, was born.

He was a chubby boy, with white skin and brown hair, soon to have the same curls as his mother, big grayish-blue eyes, a crybaby with a temper, but adored by his parents. The first great-grandchild, the first grandchild, a boy, what more could one ask for? Well, not much really.

I must make a brief but pleasant digression from these events, because I left it until this moment to tell you something very important about the life of their firstborn, Manuel. Don Armando, when some time had passed after being widowed, had contracted a second marriage with Doña Constanza. Her father had a pension, and she was very intelligent and knew how to get by in life. And the fruit of that marriage was Aunt Martina.

Well, when little Manuel was born, both Aunt Martina and her mother, Constanza, went crazy over the little boy, such being the love they had for him, that he spent more time with them than in his mother's arms. Even more so when, just over a year later, Angela became pregnant with her second son, Juan, who just like his father Samuel, was blond as wheat and with *compelling* blue eyes.

The point and the importance of this paragraph lies in the fact that Manuel adored his step-grandmother and his aunt so much that he grew up without realizing that he had more attachment to them than to his mother. But this, far from being an object of discord for marital or family life, was a pain that Angela kept to herself; when it's time comes it will be revealed, but now is not the time.

Chapter VI
The Incoherence
Of Soulless Lives

We have reached a point in history that is difficult to understand, not because of the events in Spain at that time, but because of the madness that led to the Spanish Civil War. What is narrated does not pretend to be a political analysis of what happened, but rather tells of the consequences of the conflict, and the decision making that led to horror, fear and death.

Once the Second Republic was promulgated in the capital, the right, as well as the left and the center, bet on more prominent and visceral leaders. Correspondingly, much sharper electoral campaigns were run, producing the most exacerbated politicization and radicalism of the time. Madrid and its parliament became the center of political discussion of the Second Republic.

The red-hot temperature of politics was translated into the expansion and carrying of political change, in all its aspects, to the rest of Spain. Thus, the Second Republic was proclaimed in Madrid, and hours later also in other places, shoring up in the rest of the country when the dissolution of the monarchy took place. Be that as it may, it was, especially after the elections of February 1936 in which the Popular Front triumphed, a time when the discord of a society imbued with hatred and violence turned men against their own kin; and it showed no sign of dying down.

The issue was that the Government proved ineffective and unable to contain the radicalization of the political extremes, the people, attentive and frightened by so much hostility, began to suffer the first killings, fires and harassment. From July 1936, in Madrid there were disappearances and shootings between rival groups in the street; distrust between neighbors or co-workers, so that no one knew any longer who was friend or foe; and God help you if you were not as you should be, to the "*chec*". Thus, in the capital of Spain, no one was in charge, except those that Azaña called "the caciques of the rifle" who applied their own "law" and "justice".

It was not about revenge in the face of opposing ideals or praise for one's own, because, frankly, the end does not justify the means, as those who lived this story, which is narrated below, *will show*. The authentic legacy they left are the values, principles, loyalty and full love that is condensed in the letters of Samuel and Angela, letters that he sent home full of feelings that filled him with hope and strength in the face of so much barbarism.

When war broke out, the biggest fear was of the draft, when and how it would happen. But the worst was who you would have to fight with.

Here I am in front of this page, wondering what kind of freedom led them to be in one troop or another. And the answer is that "there was no freedom of choice to fight for your ideals", if you had any at all, "it wasn't up to you and it wasn't up to them".

Recruitment depended more on geography than on ideology: if a man, generally under forty years of age, lived in an area taken by the rebels, after July 18 he was more than likely to be part of the Francoist Army; whereas, if he lived in an area under the control of the Republic, he would end up fighting in the Popular Army. It was as simple as that.

Both sides used similar techniques to recruit, because they were based on pre-war guidelines. Despite possessing very different ideologies, both armies were more similar than it might seem.

Well, although we do not know the date of Samuel's recruitment, it must have been at the end of 1937, because his first letter dates from January 1938. Be that as it may, the fact is that Samuel had no choice but to fight on the Republican side, son and grandson of a wealthy and royalist family, he was involved in a war that, like all those present, brought him nothing but misfortune. A loving couple, who had fought tooth and nail to be together, had brought two children in the world, were again forcibly separated, and this time, with the fear of never seeing each other again.

"Samuel, son, a recruitment letter has arrived, they're calling you to the campaign." Don Armando struggled to tell his son.

"Father!"

"It was brought today while you were working in the pasture. And it came with an implicit threat." So, Don Armando gave him the letter, his hands still trembling.

"What did they threaten?" His voice came out broken, like a dry olive branch that sounds when it breaks.

"If you don't show up in twenty-four hours and fight, bearing in mind that the rebels are the enemy, they will come for your wife and for me."

"Father, we have known since the war broke out that, sooner or later, I would be called up, and I must accept my fate without any feeling of guilt or blame. You must know that as long as I am at the front, they will never be able to say that you, my wife or my children can be harmed, no matter my true feelings."

"My son, how much we still have to go through!" he said hugging him.

"Father, don't be sorry. If I am honest, I am afraid, but this time, my fear is greater for you than for myself. Thinking about it coldly, the rebels know what we are like, many are friends, and I presume they will not do you any harm, as for the Popular Front, I will be in their fight and I will do what I have to do to take care of you. But, father, promise me that you will defend my family with all your vigor and bravery, as if there were no more earth or sky. This bull is hard to fight, but we will survive all this, even if we falter in the attempt a thousand times. You know how much I love Angela and that I adore my children, the fruit of my loins, do not allow them to go hungry. Do what they tell you without complaining, but always keep something hidden so that there is always a crust. And keep your weapons ready in case something happens."

"You are my life, including Angela, who has shown me during all these years *that there is no other woman braver or more forward-thinking* than her! You couldn't have chosen better, my son."

"I have to tell her, father. I have to be calm and brave so that she doesn't feel the panic that runs through my veins right now."

"Drink a brandy that'll temper you!"

"No, father, there's no brandy that will take away my uneasiness and fear that something will happen to you, which is worse than going to war."

"Go in peace and tranquility. Your father is here."

He left the winter room and asked Ramona where his wife was. She was changing their son's clothes. Juan, who was always getting up to tricks, was a blond boy with a curl on his forehead, which gave him an air of a little devil, and two sky blue starry eyes that disarmed everyone.

"Angela, what are you doing, my darling?"

"Well, since your son Juan is such a little rascal, he went into the cupboard and I caught him with one hand full of lumps of sucked sugar and in the other a sausage in oil that he had taken out of the jug, so I had to change all his clothes. What's wrong, my husband? If the face is the mirror of the soul, yours has fled! Let me lull Juan to sleep, and I'll leave him in his bassinet."

"Angela, come up to the roof terrace with me. It'll be quiet there on the wooden sofa, the one with the sheep's wool cushions, like when we used to go up there when we were newlyweds so that my father or grandfather wouldn't hear our passion."

"Now?"

"Yes."

"Angela, kiss me, with all your being and soul, with all your strength, with all your race. Give me that kiss that is never forgotten, that is kept in the depths of the heart, that is embedded in the marrow of the bones and gives warmth to the body in such a way that even cold is able to burn."

"Samuel, what's gotten into you?"

"Kiss me, Angela, and give yourself to me as if it were the last time."

Saying goodbye without knowing if you will return; saying goodbye without knowing what your destination will be; saying goodbye without knowing where you will go; saying goodbye knowing that you are leaving them alone when you feel responsible for all of them. And Angela, alone again, with two small children, at her in-laws' house, not knowing if he would ever come back.

The feeling of loneliness, fear, anguish and panic that would invade them, just imagining it makes my heart break. But they got on with it, bravely beginning the new journey of misfortunes.

The first letter reads as follows:

January 1938.

Dear and beloved wife, I hope you, our dear children and other family are well. I remain well and constantly thinking of you. It has been about a month since I left and still have not heard from you.

I have already written five letters, imagine how upset I am, because my head is in torture, guessing the thousands of things that could have happened to you. Perhaps they have not reached me because we have been moved again. When I wrote you the previous letter, we were in the trenches, but don't worry, we were thirty kilometers away from the firing line; to be in the front line would be to have only bad cards to play. I wish they would leave us here as there is a small town nearby to which we escape to buy some little things to make extraordinary meals, as my grandfather would say, "with substance", because almost always, there are no rations.

I didn't receive a letter from your brothers either, you can tell me if your brother Pedro, the baker, is at the front.

Angela, how are the babies? If it is possible for you to approach the photographer and have a picture of taken of you, because I want to see you so much that I can't help it if I get a pang in my chest.

I can't stay any longer, I must write to my parents and sister. Give my love to your brothers, sisters and brothers-in-law. And you receive a big hug from your husband who loves you and wants to see you very soon. Finally, give many kisses to our children from their daddy.

Dear parents and sister, I hope you are all well. I remain well and looking forward to seeing you. The other day I saw one of our people that I did not know, but when we realized that we were neighbors, it gave us great joy. His name is Juanito and he is the nephew of Brígido, that tall old man who passes by our door with his little donkey. His nephew asks me to please ask you to give his uncle his best regards and tell him that he is well and that he is in the fortifications. He does not know how to write so I promised him that you would tell his uncle.

I must say goodbye now; remember me to all the family, and you, my dear parents and sister, receive a big hug from one who loves you, your son, Samuel.

Isn't it beautiful? What a subtle way of not hurting the feelings of its recipients! Samuel expresses no fear, takes the heat out of being in the trenches or going hungry, even dedicates kind words to everyone and cared for a stranger. Would I do the same? May my sorrows be lessened to help bear the sorrows of others. Generosity and love.

And then Samuel got his long-awaited answer.

Bellavista de la Jara, January 2, 1938.

Dear and beloved husband, I hope you and your good friend are well, if it has been possible for you to do so. I remain well as do our dear children and other family and thinking of you every moment, not as you may imagine, but because every second I pray that God will protect you.

You tell us that you have written five letters and they have all reached us, but I am very unhappy that mine have not been received. In them I told you how our Manuel tries to write, and how Juan continues to make his mischief in the cupboard, even though there are no longer so many things to suck on. But don't get upset, there is enough to meet the needs of each day; what's more, I go every day to help my sister-in-law with the baking since my brother is also at the front. I make sure I can take two or three loaves of freshly baked bread in payment. There are days when I exchange them for some chickens or laying hens, but they are so scared that neither the hens nor the old ones are worth it.

In the last letter, I sent you a portrait of the whole family, but as you tell me that you have not received it, I will ask your father to have another one made.

We have already sent greetings to Juanito's uncle on his behalf, he was very happy, since he did not know how to get in touch with him and felt unhappy and distressed at not knowing anything. I have told him that I will write to him on his behalf and that he will surely get some other soldier to answer for him, perhaps it will be you, my husband!

Best regards from my brothers, sisters and brothers-in-law. And you receive a big hug from your wife who loves you and wishes to see you soon. Finally, Manuel sends his dad many kisses.

Angela

It echoes in my mind again, "I want to love like this, feel like this, love like this and feel like this".
Second letter from Samuel.

Dear and beloved wife, I hope you are all well. I remain well and can't stop thinking about you. I received your letter of December 27, and you cannot imagine the level of happiness that assaulted me when I receive your letter, it is as if I had eaten the best banquet in the world, because it fills my body and soul, oh, my life!

Regarding what you told me about the soap, I did not throw it away, but I forgot to give it to my cousin Maria. The trip was very hasty, so when we passed through Toreja, I exchanged it for tobacco, because from here it would be impossible to get it to you. Don't think that I wasn't also very upset, because I *know* how much you need it, but what can we do if what is done is hopeless! You tell your little brother that I am very happy to have him in Bellavista de la Jara, and that, please, in his free or lost time, he should help my father, because there is a lot of work in the fields for him alone, and every little thing that can be done is so that you can live as well as possible.

You have no idea how happy I am to know that our baby boy, Juan, is already saying "daddy", if you knew how much I want to see you, to hold you three in my arms... and my eldest, my Manuel, just imagine, already trying to write, he must become a good scribe, so do everything possible so that he learns soon and is able to write some letters for me, and please, do everything possible to take your portrait even if you have to go to Castellar.

Today, Epiphany, the feeling is even worse than the rest of the days, we are all like lone wolves; some complain about life, others prefer not to talk, others have a lost look; and I imagine you at home in the kitchen with our children, cooking those stews of yours that just by smelling them raise a dead person, and telling the kids those stories that only you know how to narrate while I'm sitting next to a fire in an oil drum. Angela, do not allow yourself to be sad, do everything possible so that our children grow up smiling, avoid fear and comb your jet hair every day, I 'can't wait to see it, touch it, comb it.

Give lots of love to your brothers and sisters and brother-in-law. And you receive a big hug from your husband who loves you and wants to see you soon. Finally, give lots of kisses to our children from their daddy.

Dear parents and sister, I hope you are all well. I remain well and look forward to seeing you.

Father, I am aware of everything you tell me in your letters and you 'don't know how upset I am to know that you are alone with the cattle. I told Baltasar that I would pay him every three days worked, and that they would be half with the profit, but you do what you think is best.

Father, I am sending you another cigar, my pleasure would be to send you the whole pack, but I 'don't have one, and if I did, it would not arrive, so I am sending you the last one I have so that you can smoke it in the living room in your armchair and enjoy a moment of peace.

I must say goodbye now, my regards to all the family and you, my dear parents, receive a big hug from your loving son, Samuel.

Dear sister, yesterday I went to the next town to have my portrait taken and though I arrived early the photographer had already left. But you do your best to have your portrait taken, because honestly, when I see you, I imagine that everything will be over sooner and we will be able to embrace each other. Give my son Manuel a slap on the wrist so that he walks properly and behaves better. And you receive all the love from your brother who loves you and wants to see you with my son Manuel in your arms.

Samuel

Three Kings Day, without shortbreads or milk to leave for the Three Wise Men, after the arduous task of distributing dreams to every home. Days that erased smiles and drew even more loneliness.

Christmas at the front and without tambourines, with the only gift of remembrance and a longing for their loved ones, the cold of loneliness accompanied by men emptied of illusions, longing for the end of a war that would allow them to return to the warmth of what was left in their homes.

I must make a clarification, on the envelope of the letter was the following not": "just a cigarette for my father, please do not take it away".

Third letter from Samuel.

Linares, March 2, 1938.

Dear and beloved wife, I hope you and our dear children and other family are well. I remain well and constantly thinking of you. I have just arrived in Linares to spend a few days resting and I am going to move heaven and earth to go to Bellavista de la Jara, even if it is only for a day. I need to hug you all, see that you are well, and steal one of those kisses that I miss so much. If they 'don't give me leave, you know how they are' I'll let you know by telegraph, so that you and my father can come and see me here.

When we stopped last night in Cordoba, I told your sister Severiana who was staying there, to tell your sister Sara so that she and Paco could find me shelter for the next few days, so that I could rest and bathe at ease, because I am no longer even a hint of the Samuel that you love so much, my wife.

I 'can't entertain myself any longer, so give lots of love to your brothers and sisters and brothers-in-law. And you receive a big hug from your husband who loves you and wants to see you soon, hopefully very, very, soon. Finally, give lots of kisses to our children from their daddy who loves them more and more.

Dear parents and sister, I hope you are all well. I remain well and looking forward to seeing you.

I have already told Angela that I will try to go to town if they give me leave, but if I 'can't, come with her to Linares. I need some urgent things and above all I need to see you.

I must say goodbye now, best regards to all the family and you, my dear parents and sister, receive a big hug from one who loves you, your son.

Samuel

Samuel was never able to have that leave, nor was he able to go home, so he sent the following telegram:

> I've been at my cousin Alfonso's house. I'm here, come and see me and bring black pants and espadrilles, if there are any, otherwise white.

> Many kisses from your son and husband who wishes to see you as soon as possible.

> *Samuel*

I don't know if they ever met, as in fact the following letter is dated July 2, 1938.

> *Levante Army.*

> Dear and beloved wife, I just received your letter dated June 21, and I see from it that you are in good spirits with our dear children, which I am very happy about, I remain well and looking forward to seeing them.

> Angela, my life, you are not aware of the joy I felt when in the morning I received this, your letter. It had been so long since I had heard from you, I read it with more eagerness than ever, I devoured each letter over and over again, you do not know how great it is for me to know that you are safe and sound after so many long nights and early mornings imagining a thousand misfortunes.

> Angela, have you answered all the letters I have sent you? I have sent you at least six, and it is not a complaint, my life, it is a need to know how you all are doing.

That night in Linares I think was the worst night of my life, I was already promising myself to go with my cousin Alfonso to Bellavista, when at dawn the colonel told us that we were going to Levante, without protest. But don't get discouraged, we'll see each other someday, this can't last forever.

Angela, my father tells me that they have already threshed the barley and that there have been five bushels, well, it has been bad, and the wheat, he says there are only ten loads, but anyway, with that and the one from the cannon farm and what my father gets, I think you will have enough to eat all year, unless they pick it up, I would like to think, Angela, that the ones I love most in this world will not lack bread at least.

As for buying some sandals for Manuel because nothing gets to you there, I have to say that I am on a bare hill in the middle of the countryside, so I can buy little for our child. I would like not only to buy them but also to take them to him.

They are recalling us, please read these letters to my parents and sister, give them best wishes and a hug from their son who loves them and wants to see them soon, and you, my wife, give kisses to our dear children that are already anxious when I can embrace them, receive the most beautiful kiss that I can send you from here and all the love I have for you.

Your loving husband.

Samuel

I don't know if it was fatigue or perhaps fear, but more and more feelings were coming to the surface in his letters, his love is expressed in them with greater loquacity. And I think I understand that it was because it was his destiny to have been on campaign since the end of July 1938,

Campaign, October 10, 1938.

Dear and beloved wife, I have just received your letter and I see from it that you and our dear children are well, which I am very happy about; I remain well and very much looking forward to seeing them.

As far as I can see, the sending of letters and their reception is going well. Please don't let the flow slow down, because feeling you and the rest of the family close to me is my strength.

We are tired, cold and hungry; if I were in the rearguard, I could fetch you the threads and tobacco for my father, as well as anything else you might need, but in these bare hills, I despair.

So many months without seeing you, without hugging you, it is dreadful, in the hours of solitude, which are many, I try not to think, I look for company to talk about anything; I don't care what, to keep you kept in my heart and without thinking about you, so it seems that I have you safe from any evil.

Angela, remember what I told you when I went to war in case something happened to me, always remember it and do what I told you, don't doubt it for a moment.

But it is over, this is going to end and I will return home and we will raise the crops and the bulls. If we have one cow left, we will raise the cattle again, nothing bad will happen to those of us who put the sky on our shoulders.

I ask you, please, read these letters to my parents and sister, give them my best regards and a hug from their son who loves them and wants to see them soon, and you, my wife, give kisses to our dear children who are no longer anxious; I am mad with longing to hold them, and you, my Angela, receive the most beautiful hug that I can send you from here and all the love I have for you.

Your loving husband.

Samuel

Chapter VII
Answer, my dear heart!

It was one of those long days when you feel rage, pain, your soul stings, you are restless and you would like to drown out the voices that, from inside you and as if from a loudspeaker, shout things at you what you do not want to hear. Even the air he breathed bothered him; he wanted that feeling of salty tears to disappear, of distressing thoughts that weighed on every breath of air.

"Samuel, stand on my left and cover that flank on your right."

"Yes, Lieutenant."

"Be careful, the night is very dark and they can breach us from behind."

His heart was pounding in his throat. He knew it wasn't just another night. The fog was dense in places and there was no moon; he felt that any noise was a "National" coming at his back; but what the hell was he doing in a war he didn't understand, on a side that wasn't his, separated from his family and feeling fear in every pore of his skin?

In his mind he began to hum a little song, it didn't matter what, in order to keep away the thoughts that unduly came to remind him that he was afraid. It was not cowardice; it was apprehension and uneasiness because that night something was going to go down. Sleep began to weigh heavy on his eyes, those sky-blue eyes that his Angela adored so much, but he dared not close them for a moment, nor blink, because that could mean death.

The shadows in the fog at the mercy of the wind seemed like drifting souls. He thought of when he rode in the middle of the fog or the rain the pastures. But then he did not feel the smell of death and blood that came to him when he tried to make out what was behind him on the white horizon.

At dawn, the sky began to sparkle with bursts of light like furtive tears that escaped from the sky. Clinging to his *Mauser,* and feeling the cold of its metal freezing his heart, he began to shoot blindly on the order of his superior; they were very close, but where would they appear? The palpitation of his heart made him look back, but his mind forced him to look to both sides, left and right, forward and back again; in seconds he would see them and his weapon would discharge everywhere. He did not want to kill anyone, never for God's sake had he imagined himself in such a circumstance! He prayed every day, but he had to defend himself.

Suddenly there was silence, *nessun dorma,* let no one sleep, let no one leave, let no one sigh or shed a tear, let no one acclaim Heaven because life is breaking, the ephemeral delicacy of the precise moment when the bullet entered his back, passing through his organs and spitting out through his neck. The blood that, so often altered by a kiss from Angela, now spilled down his sternum reaching his bell, "My God, if it is the end, take care of them and do not abandon me at the hour of my death, because I do not want to die, I do not want to die!"

"Samuel, can you hear me"

"Yes," his head said, but he didn't know if he could be heard.

"Soldier, stop the truck with the wounded!"

"Sir, that man is about to die, I do not see where there is any space, I must not waste a place with him."

"Soldier," he said, pointing at him with his regulation weapon, "if they don't take this soldier away in the truck I'll shoot that one between the eyebrows, and then there'll be room for another one!"

"Lieutenant, there's no need to be like that," he muttered between his teeth, "you can see that this is one of those we recommend," he said, "and we've already loaded him, so, please, stop pointing your weapon at me because they go off way too easily."

Samuel, seriously wounded, thrown in the truck like a sack of potatoes, was taken to the field hospital where he received first aid: rigorous asepsis, Friedrich's systemic intervention, plugging or drainage -decline- and if deemed necessary, suppression of cleansing, moist dressings, and with all this, in a short time, supposedly improving the state and progress of the wounds.

Sheltered beyond the battalion post, was the triage and classification post where each brigade received the evacuations of the battalions. It was an isolated farmhouse, with a dirt road full of potholes and stones, but it was the only safe place to evacuate the wounded. It was camouflaged, there was a refuge trench for defense, and the ambulances and vehicles were covered with oak and olive branches.

At the triage station they gathered the wounded who fell that day, Samuel among them. They saw how the wound was produced with the left clavicle coming out through the back and touching part of the medulla. They proceeded to diagnose and plug the injury and put him on painkillers, before deciding how he was to be evacuated.

He could no longer see or hear; he had lost consciousness; he let himself be carried away off by the dream of unconsciousness, by that peace that comes from letting oneself go, who knows, whether it is in the sweet taste of death produced by the gushing emptying of one's own blood.

Only those wounded who had been classified at the brigade triage station as being in shock or hemorrhaging were evacuated to the hospital. That was how Samuel was classified, but the presence of enemy aircraft overhead made his evacuation practically impossible until nightfall, to prevent the fighters from firing on the vehicle and, as the hours went by, Samuel's prognosis deteriorated.

I think it was at dawn when they arrived at the front-line hospital -there was one per Division- which was relatively close to the line of fire. Once they read his medical report, without further ado they proceeded to operate on him, trying to make it a definitive intervention and not just another patch up. The surgery having been successful, they decided to evacuate him again to the base hospital at Valdepeñas, so that his healing and recovery could progress, as there were not enough beds for the new wounded that they had been brought; again, he was transferred by ambulance.

It is curious how, in his state of unconsciousness, he told his son Manuel that his only memory of that moment was the smell of *zotal* disinfectant; he remembered that the walls of those facilities were whitewashed with lime, and how the floor was earthen overlaid with rolls of linoleum to try to make them as hygienic as possible; he remembered how they put cloth and wooden posts so that the earth and stone debris produced by the bombardments would not fall on the bodies that were being attended, or even on the operating tables.

From these lines my thanks to those hands full of courage that in such conditions restored life not only to Samuel but to so many others. Blessed are the hands that heal and cure with love, vocation and courage!

As an anesthetic, chloroform, and without overdoing it because there was a shortage; as sedatives, morphine hydrochloride and Pantopon; against infection, antitetanic and anti-gangrenous serums. And for those who had been left with total or partial paralysis of their limbs, depending on the location of their wounds, to pray for a miracle.

"Samuel, my love, it's me, Angela."

"Mom, he can't hear us. He won't open his eyes. What's wrong with my dad?"

"Samuel, my life, my heart, I am here, my love, open your eyes, come to me, please," she said, holding his hands tightly and kissing them desperately.

"Mom, don't cry or you'll get him wet. He's asleep, it's probably because he's sleepy and he's sick!"

"Madam, please leave. The terminally ill are in this wing. You must calm down and then you may come back in."

Angela's eyes were misty with tears; her love, her husband, her lover, her everything, was leaving her for a trip from which he would not return. She was sat on a bench in that corridor that led to an enormous ward. She remained impassive, mute, dead inside; she could no longer even pray; she looked at those poor men who had lost the sense of the situation of their body; lost their sight, their hearing; lost looks, absent, depressed to the point of insanity with infinite sadness; inert bodies, statues of life, dead inside and out; faces full of shrapnel, shining with the ointment that soothed the sting of burnt bandaged skin; and that smell of blood, disinfectant and chloroform.

The frightened little boy, Manuel, looked at his mother, he was becoming one of those men with a blank stare. His big blue eyes watched her attentively, without blinking, he was not aware at his four years of age of what was happening, but he knew that his mother needed him. And without thinking he threw himself into her arms and kissed her with such tenderness that his mother came back to reality.

"Mom, I love you very much."

"Don't worry. I know daddy will wake up, he's very big and strong, he's just very sleepy."

"Sure, we're going to stop by and see him again, do you want to come with me or stay with the guys out there? Maybe that's better.

"Doctor, can I come in again, I'm calm now, I can swear it to you if necessary."

"Come in, but please try to control yourself."

The steps to the ward for the terminally wounded became endless; she wanted to bring out the bravery that characterized her, she wanted to find that strength in her body that seemed forgotten; she gave orders to her brain, I want to get there now, but it was difficult to move one foot in front of the other; she carried on her ankles the weight of one who does not want to say goodbye forever to the one she loves the most.

"Samuel, my life, it's me, your Angela, I will not be parted from you, my love, not even for a moment," she approached his right ear, speaking to him with sweetness, with that love and peace that only a woman in love knows how to do.

"Angela," mumbled Samuel.

"My God, can you hear me, my darling?"

"Yes."

"Doctor, please come urgently, my husband hears me, he doesn't open his eyes, but he said my name."

"Samuel, listen to me, I am Dr. Andrade, move your lips or your fingers for me."

"Yes," he said again in a barely audible voice.

I am not able to imagine all that Angela managed to feel in those instants, but I can compare it to the greatest joy she was capable of professing, but, even so, I think I would fall short, to think that he was fighting again to live, to think that it was her voice that woke him up from the shock, to conceive how "love moves mountains".

In the days that followed, Angela remained as a nurse taking care of Samuel and anyone else she could, listening to the sick and giving them with her voice the caress they longed for. She slept in an inn for the relatives of the sick, and every dawn, wrapped in her shawl, she went to the hospital full of love, good feelings and many stories to tell. In a short time, even the doctors and nurses would stop to listen to her stories, they would stop perceiving reality for a moment to be carried away by the reverie of her sweet voice.

In a long month and still convalescent, but much recovered, it was time to part again. The war was still raging, and the National Bloc took the soldiers already recovered from their wounds who had fought on the Republican side, from the area where Samuel was, as prisoners to Madrid, specifically, to the Las Ventas Bullring.

But this time their separation smelled of hope, of that sowing that grows in the field and moves to the rhythm of the breeze, of that open sky that lets the sun caress the face, letting out that pink warmth that embellishes it, of that heartbeat in the heart that knows that it is not a goodbye forever, but on the contrary, a see you soon, my love.

Chapter VIII
Get me out of here!

It was Victoria Kent, the first general director of Prisons, who devised the new prison building of Las Ventas, located on a plot at the end of Alcalá Street -currently M 30- and Manuel Becerra Square and Paseo del Marqués de Zafra. The prison was inaugurated on August 31, 1933, when the aforementioned director was no longer in office. But the Civil War put an end to the reforming and social ideas of Victoria Kent. The prisoners who occupied the prison were transferred to a building converted into a prison in the Plaza del Conde de Toreno, while thousands of male political prisoners, supposedly militiamen, I say supposedly, because Samuel was not, were imprisoned there because of a senseless war.

The existing overcrowding, the proliferation of contagious diseases, the lack of care and hygiene, hunger, who knows what else, made Samuel's recovery more and more precarious and regressive. The days passed without respite and he could not see any way to end that torture and return home, to the arms of his "dearest and most beloved Angela". At the end of April, as if he were an angel, Angela's brother, Pedro, the baker, appeared. Thanks to him and to a safe-conduct that I never knew from whom it came, the miracle took place. Uncle Pedro, walking through corridors, arrived at the most populated place in the prison of Las Ventas, in a huge room with hundreds of living dead people, wanting to forget unimaginable physical and psychological tortures. He was almost shouting "Samuel Almena", until he guessed that that human being in a corner, curled up in a ball was his brother-in-law.

Samuel raised his head when he heard his name, thinking that another misfortune was going to happen to him. When he saw the image of Uncle Pedro, he wanted to get up, but neither the consequences of the shot nor his lack strength allowed him to do so. It was his brother-in-law who helped him to get up, the stench of his body, the impossibility of walking, eaten by lice and his extreme thinness made him unable to show the enormous love and admiration he felt for him. He embraced him as two men embrace, looked into each other's eyes and took him away. As they passed by each guard post, Uncle Pedro would only say "he is one of us, he is a National". He took him to the house of some relatives who lived nearby, and when he managed to climb the stairs to the house, he entered and there was Angela.

"Samuel, my life!"

"Don't touch me, Angela," he said dryly and harshly, "my body is corrupted, I won't want you to caress me, please."

"Pedro, tell your sister to step aside, please, and take me to the bathroom, if you would be so kind."

"Of course, Samuel. Angela prepared his clothes and something hot to eat."

I can't for a moment imagine how painful it was for Angela, to approach her husband, the man for whom she would give her life a thousand times, and he had not even kissed her on the cheek. The harshness of his voice and the contempt of his words, but what was her failing, if all she had done was love him, care for him and desire him.

When Samuel came out to the small dining room already perfectly groomed in a suit that seemed to drown him despite having been tailor-made for him, Angela looked at him with the most tender eyes she was capable of, however, all Samuel saw in them was pity and compassion, he hated that she looked at him feeling pity. Angela remained glued to the balcony shutter, the sun gave an exquisite glimpse of her shapely body sheathed in a sky-blue dress with little white flowers, the tight waist and her low bun. She clung to the curtains so as not to fall to the floor or perhaps so as not to run into his arms; the excitement was too much for her, but he held her back.

It was a period building with high ceilings, rooms that smelled of camphor, exquisitely molded ebony wood made up the sideboard and the main table, adorned with a white bobbin lace tablecloth and handmade lace. Very slowly, dragging his leg and his left arm, Samuel made his way to the table, his brother-in-law had already pulled the chair out so he could sit down, it was then that Angela approached to serve him a nice plate of beans with partridge that he liked so much. Silence was chewed by jaws clenched tighter than when eating; the three of them moved their wrists to reach the plate and gobble each spoonful, some less hungrily than others. The bread that his brother-in-law had brought tasted like a delicacy of the gods, and Samuel asked for another piece and another, until his physical hunger was satisfied. But what was wrong with him?

When Angela went to get up to help him reach the red wine velvet armchair, her brother asked her with his eyes to stay still, and it was he who helped him. He took out a pouch with tobacco. He offered him a well-filled cigarette and offered him the tinder lighter, but seeing his lack of motor skills, he decided to light it himself and poured him a glass of brandy.

On the way back to Bellavista de la Jara, Angela felt unwanted, the two men gossiped about unfortunate anecdotes of one or the other's acquaintances, but never addressed her. So, in her pain and incomprehension of what was happening there, she kept quiet, and even pretended to be asleep for a long time to see if they would talk about something concerning her. But not even on the sly or between their teeth did they make one mention of her.

Days went by and Samuel talked to all his relatives, friends, neighbors, his children, but with Angela he was not able to. She got used to being quiet and submissive, to give him smiles instead of acrimony or disdain; she prepared his clothes and dressed him almost without touching him so as not to make him uncomfortable, she tied his shoes and tied his blond hair, graying because of the war, but she never said anything. And she continued humming little songs to her children and telling stories while mending; she continued going to her brother's oven to help him and bring home bread; and to everyone's questions, she answered that she was very happy and fortunate because Samuel was now home, drowning her sadness in the routine of believing she had been abandoned.

May was ending and Pentecost was near. Samuel entered the room and found his wife getting ready to go to the procession of the Virgin, he stood still in the doorway watching how she, with her back turned, was getting dressed, with that harmony with which she did everything, slowly, caressing each stocking and the rest of the clothes as if she was going to wear them for the first time every day. She was so careful with everything that it seemed that only love could fit in her! When she became aware of his presence, she smiled at him and approached him, she went slowly to caress her husband's face, when he pulled back, turning his face away.

"Samuel, I can't take it anymore, for God's sake, tell me what's wrong, what's tormenting your head that won't even let you talk to me."

"Angela, there is nothing wrong with me."

"Don't be a fool and tell me once and for all if you have stopped loving me. If you have, then just tell me and I'll get out of here."

"Don't talk nonsense and get ready for the procession."

"You are killing me, Samuel, with your indifference and your treatment."

"Do you want to know what's wrong with me?"

"Yes."

"This war has killed me inside, and that bullet has left me useless in every way. Satisfied?"

Angela left the room like the devil in a hurry as she put on her shawl. She didn't understand what his feeling useless had to do with her loving him. Wasn't their love more important than any act to conceive more children? Damn war!

Angela let time pass, so that everything was normalizing, that the children were adapting to the new situation and that Samuel began to not be quite so cold. When she dressed him, she patted him on the back or let her hand fall below the lapel of his jacket, small caresses barely noticeable and that made Samuel gradually lower his guard.

When the hot and sunny month of August arrived, Don Armando and his wife were in Los Baños, their daughter was with some relatives, and the children were being cared for by Ramona. Angela decided to prepare a bath for Samuel in the courtyard, she filled an iron bathtub behind the palm tree with fresh water from the well and went in search of him. Samuel, faced with the sticky heat, did not put up any resistance, and allowed himself to be accompanied by her. Delicately she undressed him, his belt, shirt, shoes, pants, underwear, a ritual that she always followed, but this time she did not look him in the eyes, she did it slowly and letting him imagine her voluptuous breasts that once drove him crazy and still did, he noticed them and felt a sharp prick inside him.

Angela gave him her hand and helped him into the bathtub, as they were alone, she also took off her blouse, staying in her combination from the waist up so she could wash him better. Samuel felt uncomfortable, but this time not because he felt guilty for somehow conceiving himself emasculated, but because a kind of butterflies fluttered around his belly, but he knew he couldn't get an erection, and he felt awful and victimized.

She began to whisper an old love song, one of those ditties she loved so much, and as she poured more buckets of water into the tub, the more the fabric of her clothes got wet, until she was unintentionally soaked almost entirely, her breasts being at that moment fully admired by Samuel. He looked at her face and took his hand out of the water to caress them, and Angela, as if she were an orphaned child, took that caress with all her soul and a slight and deep smile was drawn on her lips.

Very slowly asking permission without words she was approaching his lips, then as if it were a magnet, she stuck to his mouth while her hands with the sponge cloth caressed the scar that did them so much harm, went down his neck and when she got there, she kissed it with such tenderness and desire that Samuel began to notice how a special tingling sensation ran through his crotch. Still petrified, he let his wife do what she was giving herself body and soul in every caress. He noticed in the wateriness of her kisses how little by little she was drawing him to her, how the desire and passion of times past returned in the best of gifts, Samuel felt again all the ardor in his body and the passion that had been taken away from him. He awoke from his lethargy and touched her breasts in the most perfect dance perceiving the throb of desire in every caress, he ran his hands down the beauty of her hips, beginning to desire in a crazy way to make her his again, his, his.

Chapter IX
What now!

After meeting again passionately, as is necessary between a man and a woman who, besides loving each other above all things, have gone through a war, their life went on like that of any post-war family. There was no more bull breeding: it had been annihilated. But there was still the pasture, which had to be cultivated for it to be put to use for livestock breeding. But Samuel dragged his left leg and the mobility of his arm was also impaired making it impossible to work in the field, so, with his contacts and the good quick work that characterized him, he found a position to suit him in the flour factory, although, incidentally, this did not do anything to help his weakened lungs.

It may sound strange but it is true that the couple decided to move out of the Bodegon house; to leave the family home. They moved to a house that had been inherited from a paternal uncle, cutting the umbilical cord that had woven generation after generation without a break.

It was a very special house; one of those houses with a touch between magical and somber; one of those places made of dreams. It was a house with rooms straddling the adjoining houses, something illogical for an architect today, but very common at that time, and even before. You may wonder what "houses on horseback" are, but its very name gives it away. There are rooms in the upper stories which are located over the adjoining houses, like a Tetris!

It had a wooden door, not too wide, with a golden knocker in the shape of a perfect hand, always shiny and cold. The large hallway had an ideal temperature in summer and was the favorite place of the kids who spent hours there; from there a large room that led to the staircase to the second floor, the pantry, the cellar with its dark well and the firewood -where for many years an almost dinosaur-like turtle lived and hibernated, making its first outings to the outside world in the spring- the living room, where the fireplace was -with a huge flue that was always scary to look into because it seemed that a heavy hand was going to drag you inside- the small kitchen with its window to the courtyard and Samuel's bedroom at the end of his days. There were two more floors. On the next floor, there were the rooms without corridors or doors, only being separated by curtains, which gave them a lack of privacy; and a bathroom, which in winter seemed to me to be located at the North Pole. The chambers on the third floor, reached by steep stairs, with trunks full of treasures that could never be explored, were a forbidden place during childhood.

That house was on a very steep street, which led to a small square with an iron cross that the villagers always liked to look at and sit on the small bench that surrounded it. And, a little to the left, rose a steep cobbled slope that led to the most beautiful Romanesque church in the world, at least for the Almena family, because there was that lovely, beautiful face; that face which the women in this story looked at so many times; that face that they venerated with novenas; that face to which, after mass, they sang the *Salve* on Saturdays in winter; that face which the human being sees when in his prayer he feels that his Heavenly Mother embraces him.

In these years, the marriage was happy, they fitted together hand in glove, and from that love two beautiful girls were born, Fermina and Sofia. There were now four charmers, four beautiful gifts, that were the delight and folly of their parents. They liked to tell stories and jokes, but dined in silence because, as Samuel used to say, "a sheep that bleats has a mouth that goes without". And here is an anecdote: Samuel never tasted olives or cheese, because according to him, such things could not be good.

But once again their fate, latent since the war, intervened and it became evident and they had to separate as Samuel's work was not in Bellavista de la Jara. The comings and goings reappeared, as well as the letters with their painstakingly detailed grievances and the abandonment in their hearts. Angela with the children, pulling them along and doing her best to make them happy, but once again more distant.

"Samuel, I feel bad. I'm losing weight and my period has been going on for at least a month."

"Angela, you look paler and more tired. Maybe we should go to a doctor in the capital."

"I think so. It will be nothing, but I need to do something. I can't keep up with the sanitary cloths."

"Come here' I'll snuggle with you. The night is cold and I can feel your cold nose."

In a few days she had the doctor's appointment. She noticed that her weakness was increasing; she could not climb the stairs without effort; just bending down to make the beds hurt her back; and she was bleeding more and more. The visit to the doctor arrived. They both explained the symptoms and he proceeded to examine her carefully.

"Samuel, is it possible for you to travel to Madrid?"

"Yes, doctor, and if we can't I'll sell whatever it takes. But could you explain why you are asking me this?"

The months passed relatively quickly between medical tests, searching for other diagnoses, small improvements, and Samuel's absences. Her sisters arrived and, with the grandparents and her sister-in-law, cared for her until it was time for strong, definitive treatments. Although the cancer was already being treated in Madrid, the costs were excessive, so Samuel sold some land, got enough cash and looked for the best specialist.

They went to live in the house of some dear family friends - one of those old friendships that passed from generation to generation, born in the time of grandfather Emilio Almena, the home of Remedios, near La Ventas. It was a house that Angela already knew from when Samuel was released. Hopeful, the couple went to Madrid in search of the famous medication that cured ovarian cancer. But, as they still had to take care of the children and keep to budget, Samuel had to be parted from his great love, even though seeing her in such a state broke his soul. He left with mixed feelings, not knowing whether this treatment would provide a beneficial cure for his wife.

Madrid, February 28, 1948.

Dear and beloved husband,

My hope that, when you receive this letter, you and our children are well and the rest of the family. I'm well, thank God!

Samuel, I am writing these four letters to tell you that I already know the results of the tests. According to what the doctor tells me, they didn't give me what he told you but something better and if God wills it, I will be cured. The bad news is that I still have to be separated from all of you and I miss the babies so much, also my little men and you. I know that with your mother and your sister they are well taken care of, but I must admit that the distance weighs on me.

I would like you to send oil for Remedios, you have no idea how she takes care of me, talks to me and encourages me.

You don't need to come, really, from my heart, I'm fine and you are much more needed there than here. Besides' I'll let you know when I need you by my side to hold my hand.

Give many regards to your parents, your sister, my brothers and brothers-in-law, and to our children all the kisses I am able to give to this paper, which are not few, and a very big kiss for you, my husband. From your wife who loves you so much.

Angela

Samuel, the tests have confirmed what the doctor already told you, but much worse: she has third stage cancer, but Angela does not know that. With a warm embrace.

Remedios.

Bellavista de la Jara, March 18, 1949.

Dear parents,

I am glad you are well and that mother is better. We are all well and looking forward to seeing you.

Father, you don't know how upset we have been not hearing from you all this time. I beg you; I implore you to write us more often so that we may know how Mom is doing.

I am not the one at thirteen years old to tell you what you should do, but you should do what you think is best. If you must stay in Madrid, do not worry, we are behaving well and the important thing is mother.

As for the olives you ask about in your letter, I want to tell you that they are plowed and are being prepared.

Father, we would like you to spend Easter with us, but do what you think is best. Tell Mom, that the costumes that Miguel has bought us have made us very excited, and that the girls are beautiful with their aprons.

Please tell us all about Mom, we all think about her and we are looking forward to seeing her. Don't worry about us. And I ask you a favor, tell me the truth.

Your son who loves you very much,

Manuel.

Madrid, March 26, 1950.

Dearest friend and soul sister, Angela.

I will be very happy if you are better when this letter arrives. You don't know how worried I am, because Samuel has not yet replied to the letter my husband Antonio wrote to him. I understand that you will not have time and for that reason I forgive you. But I would like to hear from you, if only once a week, which is very little to ask, because, my dear Angela, if I were able to fly to your bedside by thought, you can be sure that I would. I felt calmer and almost happy when I heard that your sister Severiana was with you. I would also like, even if it were only for twenty-four hours, to be by your side, because when I wake up in the morning, my first thought is of you and I say to myself: "How I would scurry if Angela were in the sanatorium!" You know that I made three and four trips a day, if necessary, without getting the slightest bit tired, just to be by your side and share so many hours of confidences, stories and feelings as we did.

How I wish you could write me to tell me all the things like before. I beg you to dictate some letters, either to your son Manuel or whoever else, so we can share things a little while more.

My dear friend, receive an affectionate hug from your good friend Remedios, who doesn't forget you for a moment.

"Manuel, son, please read me the letter again."

"Yes, Mom, but aren't you tired?"

"No, my life, it does me good to remember Remedios. She took good care of me these last two years. Son, never forget that. You have to be grateful even if only in your mind. Every second that Remedios has taken to write to me is an instant that she dedicated to me, to my memory, to all that we have shared, and since reading is faster than writing, I hope that you will read her letter to me many times."

"As many as you want, Mom. But if you get tired I'll stop."

"How are you, my Angela?"

"Not very well, Samuel. Sit here next to me and listen to Remedios' letter, she has taken such good care of me and I am so grateful!"

"Dad, please do something. Mom is screaming in pain. Isn't there any medicine to help her? I don't want her to suffer anymore. I can't stand it. If she can't be saved, why does she have to suffer so much?"

"Manuel, you have to be strong. I want you to go up to the room and hug her, because she has something to tell you."

"I can't. I don't want her to die, Dad, I don't want her to die. This life sucks!" he finished mumbling and bowing his head.

"Manuel, shut up, and don't think about what might not happen. Come here and give me a hug. Be a man."

"Mom, Dad says you want to tell me something."

"Yes, my Manuel, my eldest, of course. Give me your hands and let me kiss them, grip them very hard.

"Do you see how tightly we're holding on? Well, that's how I'm going to hold you always, always, always, wherever I am."

"Mom, I," he couldn't even speak, "I love you, I love you more than anything in this world. Forgive me if I wasn't always by your side, if I wasn't the best son, if I ever hurt you, forgive me."

"No, my love, I have nothing to forgive, because a mother loves without limit and gives without expectation. don't ever forget that, and do the same when you have children. And 'don't forget to take care of your brother and sisters either, because you are my eldest. Manuel, let me look at you, and give me the biggest and sweetest kiss you have ever given me. Now, off you go. Be happy, because your mother will always take you by the hand and protect you as a mother always does."

"Samuel, after so many letters, after so many words, I can only think of one thing to say goodbye to you: thank you! For all these years, for all that you have made me feel, for all the love I have felt and still feel for you."

"Angela!"

"Hush, my love. Let me say goodbye in my own way."

"Yes, my life."

"I never thought you would choose me, the shoemaker's daughter, the poor girl who could neither read nor write. But you know, in your eyes I have been and I am a beautiful woman, one of those worth fighting for and letting herself be loved; you have made me feel special, like a lady, woman, wife; the way you have looked at me, is the way that can only be understood if it is with the eyes of true love. I feel that I have a thread of life left, my love, and I 'don't want to waste it. I want you to take my hands and press them tightly against your chest, just as I pressed them against you in that hospital. Don't forget me, Samuel, but don't stop being happy, I will always be by your side in each of our children. I love you, my life, I have only lived for you and I would do it again a thousand times if I lived again! Don't let go of me, Samuel."

With all the tenderness, gentleness and emotion, Samuel held her against his chest, kissing her little face and mouth, tangled in endless tears.

"I love you, Angela, don't forget to continue loving me wherever God's arms take you."

"I love you...."

And so, my most beloved and dearest Angela left forever, on May 10, 1950, in the late afternoon and at the early age of forty-one, with a husband who loved her and four wonderful children to watch grow up.

That is how she went to her eternal rest; the woman that this narrator never got to know, about whom some ladies from different social classes and one of Manuel's childhood friends, spoke to me. And they did so, not only about Angela's physical beauty and the magic of her words, but also about her kindness, freely given to anyone who needed her, when "hunger was taken away with cakes" she always had a crust to distribute.

Angela, I love and admire you, and wherever God's arms take you, don't stop loving me a little bit. Give me that gift of people, that kindness, that great virtue of loving to the nth degree, and of course, that ability of yours to put words together in the most beautiful way in the world.

Chapter X
My Sweet Ana

Ana, I can't stop thinking about you; about everything you have meant to me. Every day, every moment in which any detail brings me a memory of you; sometimes a pot with a geranium; sometimes the smell of a stew that resembles yours; sometimes a tablecloth made with your little hands, or the sieve that you bought me in Portugal; or one of those Christmas carols we used to sing as a duet in the kitchen while preparing meals for everyone. And how many times have I needed to tell you my things and to receive that hug that only you knew how to give me! None of these ever leave my heart or my mind.... It's time to find you... and you know what? It's hard for me; it's hard for me to accept that you are not there.

Sara, Toledo on August 8, 2018.

Ana was born in Bellavista de la Jara, on March 14, 1936, the second of four siblings. That could have made her feel indifferent to the rest of the world, because she was neither the oldest nor the third of the sisters, much less the baby of the family, but Ana had something special. A few months after her birth, without knowing it, she sensed that her father had left. It was not of his own free will, but as a prisoner of war. Thus, she began her life crying her eyes out for three long years. Perhaps the fear that her mother, Fatima, felt all that time was transferred to Ana, who did not stop sobbing. But then, Ana was a crybaby all her life. It was typical that she would burst into tears in response to any emotion.

Her father, Gonzalo de la Vega, was taken prisoner to the cathedral of the city of Jaen, undoubtedly for being against the Republic, but he never knew the exact reason. Perhaps the answer is that he "smelled of wax". But be that as it may, he spent three long years crammed in one of the chapels of the Holy Cathedral where the "Holy Face" is located, where he prayed with all his heart and smelled even more of wax.

Gonzalo's eyes and nose recorded the sensation of the white light that entered through the round windows in the dome, which made circles on the floor as if they were strategically placed spotlights to direct one to where the altar was. The specks of dust moved in a perfect dance according to the rhythm of the air; or the passing of some militiaman, who brought a visitor, an errand, or a document to be completed to reach his final destination. The characteristic odor of the cathedral, despite being impregnated with humanity and the stench of feces or tears, still maintained, as always, the aroma of incense, candles and exquisitely carved wood from the majestic central choir. And in that third chapel off the left aisle, as one entered through the central door, he spent three long years watching how some who were called no longer returned.

"Irene," -Fatima's sister- "the girl cannot stand up."

"Don't worry, sister, I'm sure it's the fever, she always gets the worst of it, as father says."

"Irene, father says many true things but others not so much. Please, come here. Look, she can't put her foot down, my God, call the nurse to tell us what to do! Ana, honey, stand up and come to mommy, my girl, don't cry and walk to me.

"Fatima, I'm going to get the nurse."

"Good morning, Doña Fatima and everyone, what's wrong with your child?"

"You tell us. She has had a fever for several days, and she cannot put her foot down to walk. It is as if her legs have failed her and she has a strange weakness."

"I don't see anything serious. Give her two purges for two days and she'll be fine. I don't think she has anything else."

"Gonzalo, I am uneasy about the purges. Ana is not getting better. Please, see if your cousin from the capital has arrived and can check her. He is a good doctor. After all, she has only been treated by the nurse who, with all due respect, is not a doctor, even though all of us in the village put her on a pedestal."

"Fatima, you are very obsessive, and you like drama. I don't think it's that big of a deal."

"For God's sake, either you go or my father will! This is more serious than you think, my daughter is not well, and you men in this family always think you are right."

"I think you still live in anguish because of those years, and everything makes you think the worst."

"The worst? The fact that you have been imprisoned for three years, suffering misery, does not give you the right to call me crazy. You have no idea of the fear I have suffered these last years from the effort of raising our daughters without having two coins to rub together or to shelter me. It is thanks to my father, who was not called to the front, who took the three of us in and gave us a crust to put in our mouths. You attack me instead of realizing that the fevers are so high and the purges have not improved her at all. I am livid at what you're saying."

"Tomorrow morning I'll go down to my cousin's house and ask him to come urgently so that you can be calmer and to relieve the tension, because it's too much."

Fatima was right to worry. Ana was sicker than they thought; she was diagnosed with infantile poliomyelitis, an infectious disease of the nervous system. It affects the motor neurons of the spinal cord and brain, causing muscle weakness and acute flaccid paralysis and, very often, results in deformities. Cousin Anselmo, a renowned doctor and family physician, tried, with other doctors, to minimize the paralysis by using early immunotherapy with convalescent serum; then they completely immobilized her in the acute phase of the disease; and then in the following weeks, with splints called "leg braces". So, she was carried in her splints by her parents and closest relatives for several weeks on end.

Fatima was shocked when she heard the diagnosis. Her intense black eyes, full of tears, were fixed on her husband Gonzalo; she was not "crazy and obsessive", but rather pure maternal intuition, that feeling in the heart that makes us feel that something is not right, that something else should be done or another path should be taken, had kicked in. It is not a sixth sense but, in essence, that very specific mother's love.

Gonzalo and Fatima suffered a lot, seeing their daughter tied to boards for weeks to try to make her deformity as minimal as possible. All this on top of having been separated by war; three long years of imprisonment; and, despite having farms, because of a very poor economic situation, her struggle to raise two little girls.

Ana's family was very diverse, in particular on her father's side. Don Gonzalo de la Vega was the younger of two brothers, coming from a family with potential. And as for her mother's family, Fatima de Gila, they came from a military family that was strict and little given to affection. Such was their severity, that her father, Don Antonio de Gila, cut the four sisters' hair in summer, as he thought them too pretty, so that no man would look at them. But far from achieving his goal, they were even more beautiful with their deep black eyes and angular faces, which were immensely favored by the androgynous haircut. Thus, it can be said that, although the war had diminished the estates, Ana also came from families of noble ancestry, strict in conscience and in education.

After months of anguish, Ana healed and little by little she began to walk, but her right foot was no longer the same as her little left foot. But playful and smiling, she went on with life without giving much importance to what would become a lifelong defect. Her aunt Irene, her mother's older sister, always gave her rubs of rosemary alcohol and massaged her little leg to lessen the cramps.

Ana was feisty, with a good self-esteem; she was determined and valiant; like a spinning top she never stopped, so much so, that when they went to the fields to check the crops, her father Gonzalo said that she "made two paths", because she came and went, running from one side to the other , while the others walked in one direction. Even if there was a maid at home, she liked to help with the daily chores. She would take the bundle of laundry with Luz, the maid, and go to the river to wash it, or cut the chickpeas, which were in water, into small pieces for her father's partridges; or she would roll up her sleeves for the spring cleaning; there was no question that wherever the need was on the farms, she'd be in the middle of it.

Ana smelled like spring, fresh, laughing, wild and delicate. In April, she liked to ask the cuckoo how many years she had left to live, counting each song until the bird's calls enumerated the number of years, for that day at least. She'd compete to see who could jump the highest beside a rockrose, or make the prettiest bouquet of flowers in the farmhouse. She'd help make homemade soap, and, of course, lend a hand at the slaughter, when she'd share with her sister "el ajo" -that's what the black pudding mix is called in Bellavista de la Jara- or help with the Christmas sweets like the *polvorones*, or the lunch, or the Easter flowers and donuts that took away the hiccups.

Her best friend was a first cousin, Pepita: the two little girls loved and hated each other equally, competed to see who could get the most leaves by catching them between their hollow palms, or racing each other, or who could hide better. But the fights were so constant that Fatima and Aunt Nieves decided that they would never play together again. Then the pain of separation was so great that, when they were given permission to get together again, there was never any new friction nor any voice louder than the other. They were cousins and friends for "forever and ever".

But there was another accomplice and friend, her older sister, Pilar. The two sisters sheltered and helped each other. They liked to sing during the siestas, and to make up dramas, in which they imagined being the heroines of some of the movies they saw for free from selling tickets in the back room of a house opposite the cinema. Though they were talkative among themselves, telling each other their little secrets, outwardly they were the epitome of rectitude, fruit of that strict and weighty education which emanated from a chain of values and behaviors rooted in previous generations.

How different Ana was when socializing with her elders. If she had raised her head, more than one of them would have suffered a serious turn, she told me with a laugh. In the summers, as a girl, she had the ritual of sitting at the door of her Aunt Irene -a lady from head to toe but with an uncommon pragmatism- and, every afternoon, she would pick unopened jasmine buds, take a safety pin or long pin and string them together, and once fixed, she would pin her jasmine bow to her chest.

Jasmine was the favorite scent of her childhood, because Ana also repeated this ritual, not only on her breast, but also put them next to the little Virgin that she had on her bedside table. Well, Ana would sit at the door, and everyone would say hello to her. If they were not very well known, or a stranger, they would give a polite greeting, but if they were family, of course, it was quite different. They would give her a kiss and a hug, and ask about the state of health of all the relatives, including Uncle Menganito, who had moved to Valencia twenty years ago! But then came the real fun, the anecdotes. She loved that part, because even though she only knew two or three characters in the story, they were always very entertaining, and if any of them had a little bit of infatuation or mischief, then the evening became a very special moment.

In addition to the doors of relatives and close friends, there were the doors and windows with curtains, behind which the occupants knew all the gossip. Ana knew that, if you passed one of those doors or windows with a companion, by the time you reached the corner of the street even the prompter knew about it, the information having arrived faster than a telegram. And on returning to home sweet home, the socialization and gossip would have taken its toll on her mother and father, whose interrogation shook her and took from her mind the sweet moments she had just enjoyed. In short, the boundless Ana had arrived just before the war and grew up in the austere post-war period, but neither one thing nor the other, nor her lameness, dampened her will to live.

Chapter XI
Who do you think you are?

"Mother, did I braid my hair properly? And did I tie the red ribbons properly?"

"Ana," she said with a certain jaded tone, "you look perfect."

"It's my first official tea, and you know that Josephine has a dream house. Her father is a county judge and is a very important man. He has an imposing mustache that curls upwards, like a buffalo!"

"Ana, they are people like everyone else, no more, no less, and don't make fun of them. Let's see what shoes you put on."

"Laced boots, mother. But I've cleaned them and they're squeaky."

"Watch you don't stain your dress, I know you!"

"Mother, thank you for letting me wear my Sunday dress. This lace is so lovely. Look, when I turn around it flies like a parasol. Aunt Irene says I look like a meringue," she laughed.

"Anna, we are all equal in the eyes of God, but you in the eyes of others?"

"What's wrong with me? Do I look ridiculous?"

"No, my daughter, you're a doll, but those boots..."

"With them I can run, in case we play in her garden, have you seen it? I love the palm trees along the walk to the fountain with the angels, and those carved stone benches. What's the name of that stone? Marble? I feel like a princess, what time is it?"

"You still have half an hour left. It's not good to be late, but it's not good to show haste either. You're so impulsive!"

"I'm so happy, I could fly and float. Look at me, mother!"

"It's just that those boots...," She looked at her with compassion and some pain.

"But they're the most beautiful boots in the world, Mother. I bought them with the two pesetas that Grandpa gave me at Three Kings Day and for my birthday. Besides, I'm as fast as the wind with them. Don't you like them?"

"No, daughter, you are right, they are the most beautiful boots in the world and no one wears them with more style than you do."

"Do I get a kiss, Mother?"

"Ana, don't be daft. You know that kisses are nonsense, manifestations of weakness. The important thing is to make yourself respected. And I hope there won't be any amorous chitchat."

"No, Josefina only invited girls."

"I hope I don't hear different!"

"Do I look pretty? Perfect?"

"It's time. Go now and be home by six o'clock!"

Ana hopped down the street from her house, humming one of those little songs she used when playing: "*Teresa the Marchioness, chiviri chiviresa, she had an altar boy, chiviri chivirillo, and a priest sacristan chiviri chivirán...*" The road was very long, she passed in front of the market place where the vendor was preparing the dough for the *churros* while he sang *fandangos*, and then she passed in front of Aunt Irene's house.

"Should I stop to say hello? What if I'm detained? I'd better not. I'll see her on the way back."

It was four o'clock in the afternoon when she arrived at Josefina's gate. She was so nervous that she thought about knocking on the service door, but then she remembered that she had an official invitation so, she rang the bell at the entrance.

"Good afternoon, Miss Ana. Come in."

"Good afternoon."

"Miss Josefina is waiting for you in the solarium. She is with her mother cutting flowers to decorate the coffee room."

"Am I the first to arrive?"

"Yes, Miss Ana, you are the first. You are very punctual."

"My mother says that one shouldn't be late because it offends those who are waiting, but one shouldn't be hasty either because then everyone will see how anxious you are," she answered with a laugh.

"Go through that door and the entrance to the solarium is to the left."

"Good afternoon, Doña Enriqueta, and to you, my dear Josefina. I hope you are happy to see me!"

"Of course, dear Ana. We are delighted to have you in our home. By the way, you look very pretty, just like a china doll."

"That's what I said to my mother. This dress is the most beautiful I ever had. The fabric was bought for me by my aunt Irene in the capital. She travels a lot because she is the agent of the Banco Hispano Americano. My mother did the sewing, and her needlework is magical."

"Well, a little princess like you is worthy of such a dress."

"Mom, would you excuse us? It's a beautiful spring afternoon and I would like to take a walk in the garden with Ana. Besides, the day after tomorrow is Ana's birthday and I want to give her a present."

"Of course, daughter, go on, I'll finish the posy."

After walking through the garden, smelling Doña Enriqueta's red, velvety roses, they arrived at the eucalyptus tree that sheltered an iron cross. The girls sat next to it, on one of those benches that seemed to be made of bobbin lace, and wrote their names in sand with twigs. Self-absorbed, they talked childishly about how they would be when they grew up.

In the back wall, which was covered with thick ivy, there was a wide barred window, which had no glass, with two rings on each side for the hitching of horses. It was rather a kind of giant spyhole to check out any laborer who wanted to access the house by the carriage gate. And there, peering in, was Manuel with his big blue-gray eyes, totally absorbed, staring at Ana like an imbecile. She felt how the blood rose in her whole body and rushed to her face until her ears burned. However, at the same time, her honor made an unusual courage rise from her feet, she could not allow anyone to look at her that way.

"Hey, you! What are you looking at? Do I have monkeys on my shoulders or are you just catching flies?"

"Forgive me, I didn't mean to intrude. I just saw the two of you by accident. I hope I didn't disturb you."

"Hello, Manuel, how is your mother doing? I know from your father that things are not looking good".

"Thank you for asking, Josefina. She is quite ill, and the pains are so intense that she can hardly bear them. So, I went for a walk and when I saw you, I felt happier."

"Ana, do you know Manuel Almena?"

She wanted to become invisible, to cease to exist, for being a fool, for being mouthy, for being impulsive; her mother was right, "quiet is prettier".

"I'm sorry to have frightened you. I'll let you enjoy this beautiful spring afternoon. I'm going to keep walking in search of my father, who'll be in the pasture. My mother's brother, Uncle Pedro, has come, and they've gone for a walk too."

Ana's world changed dimension. She had never felt like this before. She had never imagined that just one look from Manuel could suddenly produce so many sensations. Why couldn't she stop thinking about him? She didn't care for layabouts. Besides, her mother had always told her, it was a sin; it was forbidden to think about a layabout. But this one, embedded like a constant echo, wouldn't leave her mind.

"I've had enough! Am I crazy? Blessed Virgin, help me!"

She felt a tingling that ran from her belly to her throat. She had no eyes or ears for anyone else, and the magic of the invitation to have tea paled against that moment in the garden; that moment in which he looked into her eyes. She saw in them a strength that transformed him; the attraction that provoked the desire for him not to stop looking at her, which the depth of those pupils filled with the sadness that was in his heart due to his mother's illness was emphasized; and for the first time she discovered the beauty of that face.

But at the same time, she felt violated, both in her body and in her heart. "What is wrong with me?" she asked herself when she returned home. She was experiencing a strange sensation of mistrust, joy and guilt, the fruit of a religion based on a very narrow conscience, but she could not stop thinking about him. Her mother first said that there was no one, but she kept thinking about those blue-gray eyes and the curly black hair of the most captivating lad in the world. And remembering the harsh words she spewed in response to that precious look, "And you, what are you looking at, do I have monkeys on my shoulders, or are you just catching flies?" hammered in her head.

Ana arrived home at six o'clock sharp, neither before nor after. She had wanted to tell Aunt Irene what had happened to her, but she dared not be late home. So, she crept in. But her mother, Doña Fatima, was sitting in the rocking chair in the hallway, waiting for her little girl to get home. The first thing she did was to ask her how it had been, what they had eaten, and how Doña Enriqueta was. Then she instructed her to get changed and to leave her dress hanging neatly on the clothes rail in her room. Ana did so. She changed slowly, so unusual for her that even her mother wondered why she was taking so long. She was going through moods that she had never experienced before: euphoria, fullness, harmony, frustration. Then Ana came down the stairs pouting, humming a song, self-absorbed and not very expressive.

"Ana, who was there?"

"Josefina and I, her cousin, Araceli, the nurse's cousin, and Marujita, Aurelio's cousin."

"You've put the cart before the horse. But don't worry, Ana. The 'I' always comes at the end."

"I'm sorry, Mom. I'm tired and don't really feel like talking."

"Did something happen to you at Josefina's house? You're acting all weird, daughter."

"No, it's just that..." said Ana with a crestfallen face.

"What? Don't give me one of your father's silences. You know how nervous they make me."

"That maybe I had higher expectations, and I thought I was going to have a better time."

"That's why you shouldn't go to places with a preconceived idea. It'll only leave you feeling dissatisfied or disappointed and ruin the pleasure."

"Mom, I'm going to sleep, or at least to lie in bed, as I've got a bit of a headache."

"Go on, go. I'm sure it will do you good. A rest is always beneficial."

Ana daydreamed in her bed, even though she knew it was a sin to think of him; but his gaze had pierced her, his tyrannical words had punished her; and without understanding why, she only wanted to fall asleep fantasizing about his eyes.

Ana, it was not a sin to sigh while daydreaming, because that sigh and image were accompanied by innocence and purity. Your new love was full of sublimity and sensitivity, and that precise moment when Manuel looked at you, was a little piece of happiness that you have remembered all your life.

"Ana, wherever you are, don't stop dreaming...."

Sara.

Chapter XII
The first letter

Ana, dazed and absorbed in her own awakening to love, ignored the things that were happening around her. If her mother sent her to the shop to get a piece of bacon for the stew, she brought homemade soap and start washing; if she had to put in order the clean clothes that Luz had brought from the river, she folded them without ironing them; if she had to help in the housekeeping chores, Ana started dancing in front of the mirror: it was nothing more than daydreaming.

Her thirteenth birthday arrived. She was very happy, that day her mother was going to make her favorite meal and go to the oven to knead and bake the dumplings that she liked so much. She got up grinning from ear to ear. Her sister hugged her and then everyone else at home, except her father, who was already at the cooperative making the samples of olive oil that were going to be collected by the community members and other customers. As Uncle Pedro's oven was on the way, she stopped by to see her father, shyly and respectfully entered the laboratory, hugged him and was reciprocated with a sweet kiss on the forehead and a coin to buy lupins in the market.

While she was kneading the dough with her mother and her Aunt Pilar, filling each other's nostrils with flour and giggling over the smallest detail, they sang fandangos and folk songs in a duet. Then Aunt Pilar whispered in her ear,

"You are very giddy, girl. Butterflies are fluttering around you." Anna, red and bothered, glared at her sister as if she wanted to kill her, said haughtily,

"It's you who has a *lover* who makes ruts going up and down the street to see you."

Then Fatima frowned, and in a voice almost inaudible to the rest of the universe, devoted some harsh words to them,

"If you so much look at a young man, or let yourself be looked at by one, you won't ever go out for the rest of your life." They both bit their tongues and made guilty gestures to each other.

After the family lunch and the birthday celebration, Ana asked her mother for permission to take a walk with Josefina and Marujita.

"Josefina, do you have a moment?" Manuel asked.

"Sure."

"I have a favor to ask, but I almost don't dare."

"Tell me, Manuel, if it is for the best, count on me."

"I don't know whether the consequences will be good or not, but I have a confession to make."

"Now, you're making me very nervous, Manuel. Spill the beans."

"Remember the other day at your house, when you introduced me to Ana?"

"Yes, how could I forget. She fell into a perpetual trance," she said to herself.

"Well, I haven't eaten or slept since that day. She's like an angel fallen from heaven, with her pretty smile and her braids, her boldness and disdain. I need you to give her this note. I ask for your complete discretion, not only for her sake, for I do not wish to cause her any harm, but also for her family. I haven't put anything in that is not true, just the admiration I have for her."

"Manuel, I don't like playing matchmaker, but since Ana and her sister are very protected and restricted, I will do you the favor. Today is her birthday, so I will see her shortly. The only impediment is that Marujita, the nurse's daughter, is coming, but I will do my best to try to get alone with her. How is your mother?"

"I have just come from reading a letter sent to her by a great friend of hers in Madrid, and from writing her an answer. They don't tell me the whole truth, but I know that my mother will be leaving this earth very soon. I am very grateful to you, Josefina."

"You're welcome. Go with God."

The document in question was a hybrid between a note and a letter, because it was longer than a note but too short for a letter. Ana always told us how it happened, but never the content. According to her, Josefina asked her to enter her house because she had something to give her, and she kept Marujita out of the way by telling her it was an errand that Doña Enriqueta was going to do for Doña Fatima. They entered the immense hallway and she took her by the arm, going up the main staircase like lightning, they entered Josefina's room and closed the door cautiously. Josefina opened her bureau and, from a hidden drawer in the back, took out a small envelope. She handed it to Ana with a wink, telling her it was a letter for her. She opened it slowly, as if the contents of the envelope were going to sting her, took out the sheet of paper and read it to herself. Josefina questioned her with her eyes, but Ana said nothing. Then she took the sheet of paper and read aloud,

Miss Ana, I take the liberty of writing you to confess that my heart never stops beating for you.

Sincerely yours, Manuel Almena.

"But who does he think he is? He's a scoundrel who thinks that because he's the son of an important family, we're all going to follow him like ducklings behind their mother. Not even in his wildest dreams!"

"Ana, how can you say that? What he says is sincere and very nice. I don't think he is either a scoundrel or conquering, and much less with what is happening to him at home. What's more, I think it's beautiful that on your birthday you receive a letter like that. What more could you want?"

"Josefina, don't say that! I'll get into trouble. If my mother finds out about this, she'll put me in a convent for life! Besides, thinking about him is a sin. Yet I can't top thinking about him, even though I'm condemning myself more and more; no matter how often I pray the act of contrition, I can't get him out of my head. Tell him that I do not want his note, nor do I wish to know its contents, and that he should not look at me or come near me."

"Are you sure, Ana?"

"Totally. I've got to go, I'm running late. Bye, Josefina."

Ana, more obstinate than a mule, was in denial. Her outburst was remarkable. She "asserted herself", as she said, because one can never give a "yes" lightly without seasoning it. The decency of a woman is measured by her actions and her words, and if she had answered Manuel, he would have believed her, and then soon forgotten her. Ever since she was a little girl, she knew she was different, with a special gift that made her completely unforgettable. But the aftermath of machismo and a strict upbringing meant that women could not allow themselves to be admired, flattered, much less desired.

Manuel and Ana met from time to time on the street, furtive glances, excessive and bumptious laughter. Manuel began to court Sarita, a pretty and congenial young woman, with whom he strolled through the garden and the main square. One afternoon, when Ana was with her friends, Josefina and Marujita, she saw the couple turn up, and again, that inner heat that made her stomach turn inside out, along with the desire to tell herself some home truths about the impotence of "asserting herself". However, she could not help herself and began to sing a little ditty to her friends while looking at the couple: "*The boy Manuel and Fernandito's daughter are already coming, mark their little step.*"

Her friends roared with laughter at the couple and Sarita, all proud, haughty and wound up like a spring, took Manuel's right hand. But disturbed and nervous by what was going on around him, and no doubt not wanting to hurt Ana or to look bad with Sarita, he abashedly let go of her hand. Sarita in an outburst of jealousy, turned and planted one of those loud kisses on Manuel's cheek. Then Ana, half turned, and laughing with her friends, ignored Sarita's frivolous retaliatory look. But, deep in her heart, she jeered at Manuel's oafishness with all her might.

Summer passed; winter passed; spring arrived, and with it arrived Angela's death. It is curious how life marks unions and inseparable bonds, so the first person who visited after Angela's last breath was Ana's mother, Doña Fatima.

Manuel, now fifteen – thinking he was a man but still a boy – was lost in the pain of his mother's death; and, due to the advice of friends, was in no man's land. He let himself be loved by the sweet girls of his age, who admired him and wanted to console him, and bore the sometimes painful silences of his father Samuel.

That summer, Ana began to wear her hair in a different style: long and half-curled and adorned with beautiful bows. One afternoon in the strong August sun, after exchanging countless little glances with Manuel, she let him know indirectly that she would be going up to her teacher's house around six that afternoon, as she had been invited, along with other pupils, to have tea. To get to Doña Petra's house one had to go up one of two very steep slopes, but between them, there was a not very busy alley that connected them. Ana supposed that, if Manuel knew she was going to Petra's house, if he wanted something from her, he would meet her in that alley, since the other two slopes, besides being crowded, had both Manuel's and her relatives as residents.

Ana got dressed slowly. She put on a sleeveless, red and white striped dress, which was tight at the waist and had a boat neck; a pretty frilly petticoat; and the white espadrilles with red bows that Aunt Irene had given her. She folded the red chiffon scarf she'd got for her birthday and carefully put it on her head, leaving her long brown hair underneath, which made her sweet and smiling face even more noticeable, as well as her first freckles. She liked to be flirtatious and feminine in the sun. She took the bottle of jasmine perfume that she shared with her sister, and with great skill, put a few drops on her wrists and behind her ears, which was enough: "everything in its right measure". She could not abide excessively strong smells. She went downstairs and went straight to the living room to obtain the approval of her parents. Both contemplated her slowly. Just as her father was about to speak, her mother, Fatima, came forward, and gave her own threatening instructions and warnings. Then her father drew her to him, contemplated her and kissed her on the forehead, the way Ana liked so much, and with a simple "behave yourself" sent her on her way.

Ana looked at the grandfather clock which was chiming six o'clock. She had to leave now, she turned flirtatiously and winked at her parents and closed the hallway door to keep out the afternoon heat. She noticed how a slap of hot air entered her lungs as she tied her scarf and began her planned itinerary. Now her mind did play tricks on her. She wondered if Manuel had understood her intention; if he would appear along the way and say something; if he really loved her or just saw her as an amusement, if her mother would find out... enough! She caught herself talking to herself in the street; folk were going to think she was out of her mind.

The heat made the slope even steeper, and the waistline stuck to her beautiful body, but then she remembered what Aunt Irene always said, "climb like an old man and you'll get there like a young man", so she slowed her steps and took a deep breath. Without realizing it, she entered the alley of Las Animas. Suddenly, it occurred to her that she might meet Manuel. Her heart began to beat like crazy, an emptiness in her stomach took over her breathing, and she felt uncontrollable nausea. Then, suddenly, at the beginning of the curve, there was Manuel, leaning against the wall with one foot dirtying the white wall of the notary's house, wiping his forehead with his handkerchief. He was wearing a white shirt, with the black crepe on his left arm, and a pair of charcoal gray pants.

"Good afternoon, Ana," said Manuel with a broad smile.

"Good afternoon, Manuel. What a coincidence finding you here," commented Ana, lowering her eyes slightly.

"Sometimes there are coincidences. May I use the familiar form with you? The truth is that I knew you would come this way to go to Doña Pera's house. Marujita told me you'd be coming too. This is the shortest way, but also the steepest."

"Of course, Manuel, you can be familiar, we've known each other for a long time."

Manuel took a step towards Ana, who was petrified, unable to move a muscle in her body.

He took a deep breath. The heat was suffocating, but the feeling that was running wild again was even more so. His heart was beating non-stop, his hands were sweating, he was trembling inside, but he had to tell her what he felt. He had to do something now. Without any further ado, he closed his eyes and approached Ana's lips, slowly, barely touching them, and without thinking about the consequences, he kissed her softly. It was one of those kisses full of love and hope, an almost imperceptible touch on the silky, full of life lips of his beloved Ana. The kiss that he had dreamed of so many times, and was able to give, had an unwelcome response, though it was none other than the one that could be expected from Ana. "To assert herself", she drew back from him, and without thinking twice, slapped him so hard that his cheek was left with the tattoo of her five fingers.

Manuel didn't know what to do. The stinging that ran down his left cheek stunned his face and his embarrassment at her response. The things he would have liked to tell her, but didn't because he contained his rage, despite the thousand and one thoughts and sensations that swirling in his heart and mind.

Ana, astonished by the unexpected kiss and the abrupt reaction of her hand, did not pause to think rationally. She pulled away from Manuel, looked at him and let her heart do its work. Then, full of passion, she grabbed the collar of Manuel's shirt and closing her eyes, full of love, she melted into the most penetrating, intense, precious kiss that she was able to give; the best kiss of her whole life, because that kiss was forever the first and the most important for them. Time stopped. It was not necessary to say anything more, because it was all sealed. Their love, flowing from both bodies, cast off their "me" and transformed it into an "us". They floated. It didn't matter if it was forty degrees in the shade; if they were having tea at Doña Pera's house, if they were seen by some busybody; the fact was simple, they loved each other.

Chapter XIII
In a cloud

Ana and Manuel began their joint walk through life in secret. They met in the garden or in the square, on Sundays at mass, and exchanged notes through their friends. But they were not able to court with peace and serenity.

In view of the situation and, knowing that it would be impossible to keep their love like this, Manuel decided to do something. It was August 15, the Feast of the Assumption of the Virgin Mary, who, for both of them was so present in their lives. He shaved, put on cologne, put on a clean shirt, polished his shoes and left his father's house at two o'clock in the afternoon. The sun was beating down like a hammer and it was scorching, but his hands were cold, unlike his mind which was a hotbed of thoughts. His step was firm, sure, determined, but when he tried to say a word out loud, his throat was dry as a stone and his voice cracked. But that didn't matter because he was going to do it anyway.

He arrived at his destination, stood in front of the door and without thinking about it, he took the knocker and gave two sharp raps. He waited for a few seconds that seemed like hours, when suddenly Luz, Ana's maid, came out.

"What can I do for you, Master Manuel?"

"I would like to speak to Don Gonzalo, if that's possible?"

"They are eating their fresh cucumber gazpacho now, so I don't know if it's the most advisable thing to do."

"Please, Luz."

With an expectant face, a "what's going to happen" grimace and a mischievous grin, she entered the room ready to proclaim loudly:

"Don Samuel Almena's son, you know, Master Manuel, is at the door, with a besotted look, asking to talk to you. Will you see him? I have already told him that you are eating fresh cucumber gazpacho, but he is most insistent, and it is not my place to say yea or nay, just to pass on a message. What shall I tell him?"

The spoons fell with maximum gravity on the plates of all those present. Ana, who at that moment had just put her spoon in her mouth was neither able to swallow nor spit out its contents. Her mother looked at her wide eyed; her sister Pilar gave Ana a kick which she did not even feel; the younger brother burst out laughing, and Fatima, without hesitation, gave him a clip on the ear that almost sank his head in the bowl.

Slowly her father Gonzalo, with his napkin hanging from the collar of his shirt, got up, cleared his throat to make his voice as gruff as he could and walked meditatively towards the door of the living room. Not a fly could be heard, everyone was goggle-eyed, except for Ana, whose jaw was digging into her chest, not even daring to breathe.

"Good afternoon, Manuel. What brings you to my house at this hour to break the respectable lunch hour? Don't you eat?"

Manuel, red as a tomato, stammered,

"I am here...."

"Spit it out, Manuel, my gazpacho is getting warm."

"All right. You know that I love your daughter, and if you didn't already know it, that's what I'm telling you now. I really love her, and I want your consent to formally let her be my bride. I don't want to hide. Besides, it's not manly to do so."

"And you come at this hour to tell me such a thing? Haven't you been taught at home to respect the sacredness of lunch?"

"Yes, sir, but courage comes when it come, and it came to me without food."

Gonzalo smiled inwardly, but remained impassive.

"Well, I'm only going to tell you one thing, which is that I'll sleep on it and you'll hear from me. Now go home and eat and let me do the same." Gonzalo entered the dining room, where everyone remained quiet and without eating. Ana raised her head and with her eyes full of tears looked at her father. "And why are you crying, Ana?"

"What did he want at this hour? People don't even know how to respect lunch hour anymore. Let's hear what surprise the young man had for us," said Fatima in the driest voice she could muster.

"He wants to formally court Anita," answered her father, "and I told him I'll sleep on it, so, shush. Everybody eat! Now leave me in peace, you too, Fatima."

As far as I understand, the meal was a poem. Ana was quiet, which made her prettier; Fatima fumed and glared; the siblings stifled their laughter; and Luz sang a refrain as she went back and forth to bring food for the rest of the lunch.

When lunch was over, Ana went to her bedroom like a pensive princess, but her heart was ringing with joy. Her Manuel had been brave enough to ask her father's permission. They would no longer have to hide, even if there were hardship, because now their love was confirmed and known. She lay down on her bed and let the siesta and the afternoon pass, until suddenly her mother opened the door without knocking.

"Ana, go down to the living room, your father wants to talk to you."

"Mother, please don't be angry with me."

"I am angry. Why does that oaf come to ask for anything? But your father has something to tell you." They both went down the stairs quietly, without looking at each other.

"Father, Mother told me that you were looking for me."

"Sit down, Ana. What I'm going to tell you is very important. Though commitment is a very significant thing, decency is even more important. To my mind, you are too young to have a boyfriend; you are only sixteen years old; but if that's what you really want, you may have it. Of course, I don't allow anyone to sully my name or your mother's name in the streets, so your courtship will be by our rules, which is the way it should be."

Ana rushed to her father and kissed him and gave him the biggest hug she could, then she went to her mother and kissed her, and Fatima gave a slight smile which to Ana felt like glory.

"One more thing, from now on you will meet at the door of the house, and your mother will be in the rocking-chair waiting for you. When you and your sister go out, it will be with a chaperone, and beware lest you sully your virtue."

"Thank you, Father, I will not let you down!"

And so, the days went by, and without either of them realizing it, it was Christmas. And with it, the Midnight Mass. This mass, along with the priest who celebrated it, had consequences for Ana and Manuel.

The night was cold, and after dining on the delicacies that had been prepared in both houses, Ana and Manuel dressed up and left for the church with their respective families. At the door, their fathers, Samuel and Gonzalo, greeted each other warmly, while Fatima and her three daughters went to their usual pew in the women's area. The last bell rang, and all the parishioners were ready to enter, so, in the same way, they went to sit in their usual pews, but in the men's area.

Manuel positioned himself first on the left, next to the aisle, while Ana sat in the same place, but on the right side of the pew; she with her little black mantilla and her missal; he with his suit and the black coat that his father had ordered the tailor to make for him. As the service began, Manuel's eyes were fixed on the perfect profile of Ana, who was bending her head so as to be able to turn her face for a few seconds and look at Manuel, "I look at you, you look at me, I love you, you love me".

The time for communion arrived, and both, in their respective rows, prepared to receive communion. But when Manuel approached, the priest denied him the host, requiring that, after the completion of the Eucharist, he come to the sacristy. Likewise, when Ana approached, she was also denied the host and given the same instruction. Imagine the embarrassment for them; the embarrassment for Fatima; and the gossip arising from the event caused the comments at the exit of the mass to proliferate like rabbits.

"May we come in, Don Bernardo?" Manuel said breaking the silence.

"Come in both of you and sit down. I am very angry and upset. The Mass is not the place to come to look at each other or to desire each other. You know that it is a sin, and you are in grave fault for looking at each other in that way. So, I am going to give you confession to redeem you from your faults, and then I will give you communion. From now on, you will not come to Mass together; you will come at different times."

"Forgive me, Don Bernardo, but my love for Ana is pure, genuine, and with all my soul. I do not look at her sinfully or lewdly. I look at her because I want her to be the love that will accompany me for the rest of my life, for her beauty and her virtues."

"Shut up, Manuel! The devil keeps messing with your head so that you don't realize the grave danger you run with so much love that is nothing more than carnal desire. Let's go to confession, period!"

Ana and Manuel confessed a guilt they did not feel, for their gaze was simple and full of true love, the kind of looks that give life, and making the heart fly when you feel them. But in the eyes of the priest, Ana and Manuel were guilty of carnal desire and evil.

When Ana recalled it at home, she did so with some sorrow and a little anger, because in truth, her looks could not make one think -and even less in church- that they were charged with the impure desire -according to the mindset of those times- of wishing Manuel to make her his. She had looked at Manuel completely in love.

She thought of the phrase "an impure look", a look that is always linked to sexual repression, but nothing was impure for Ana, except the prejudiced thought of that priest. Distressed, she spoke to her father Gonzalo, who with great gentleness explained to her that such looks were usually censored by those whose office was to judge, because they were previously predisposed to it. Thus, they rejected outright anything that seemed to have a sexual content, even when those looks were only charged with love. The priest's disdain, accusation and confession of a lewd look, made them believe that true love was a sin.

She fell asleep with a wish, "don't look at me with impure eyes, look at me with the eyes of your heart and you will see more beauty and love".

Chapter XIV
The lie

"Why is he lying to me?" Ana asked herself that question a thousand times.

"Manuel, did you have a picture taken with Sarita?"

"Ana, why are you asking me such a question, who told you such a thing?"

"I ask you again, did you have a picture taken with Sarita?"

"Ana, that question doesn't make sense, why would I have a picture taken with her?"

"I don't know, but I would like you to tell me the truth."

It was dusk at the beginning of autumn; the sunny days shortened and with the first rains the trees in the garden were ochre colored.

Ana, under her red umbrella, stared at Manuel, waiting for the honest answer. Her eyes fixed on his, without blinking, looking for the truth, had he had a picture taken with Sarita, yes or no. The seconds were perpetuated as a prologue to a wrong answer.

Ana kept repeating to herself "tell me the truth for God's sake", but the poison of lies had invaded Manuel's vocal cords, and then she heard a "no".

Every lie has a consequence; but knowing Ana, any path taken was going to be painful: she hated lying. In her strict and meticulous upbringing, outrages such as lying were punished excessively and, besides, if he had lied to her over a trifle, he could lie to her about anything from that moment on. Trust was lost, and the bitter poison of the lie nailed with such venom in the heart, that any antidote seemed impossible.

"Manuel, you have lied deliberately and to my face. The spiteful tongue of your dear friend Sarita spread its poison to Marujita's house and sent me scurrying to check whether it what she'd heard was true or not. So, an hour ago, I had my nose stuck to the window of the photographer's shop. You have just shown me that I cannot trust you. Doubly so. Firstly, because you flirt with others; and secondly, because you have lied to me. You didn't even have the guts to tell me something that happened innocently, or perhaps not so innocently.

"This time there is no turning back. Here, take the bracelet you gave me! It will suit Sarita's wrist better, because it burns me to the core. It took you an eternity to win me and you have lost me in the time it takes to tell a lie."

"Ana, please, it's not true. Things are not as they seem. There is always an explanation. Let me at least tell you how it happened."

"Manuel, I don't want to hear it. I asked you outright and your answer was a lie. Are you afraid to tell me the truth? Are you afraid that a truth will make me stagger? Listen to me well. I hate lies, because on top of the deception of having a picture taken with Sarita, you have added a lie. Double pain, Manuel. Why?"

"Ana, I didn't intend to be with Sarita, or to hurt you. It was really a misunderstanding. I didn't know that the photo was going to be put in the window. What happened was that I was there with my friend Paco, and he took me by the arm and put me in front of the camera. It was a childish prank, a joke.

"By God, Ana! I love you with all my soul, that I cannot be without you; you are my whole life! I want no other love than yours."

"Enough, Manuel! It's over. What's done is done. You should have told me when it happened, and you should have told me the truth. But you kept silent, thinking I wouldn't find out, and that's the way it ended. Lies have very short fuses and, before the rooster crows, they explode in the heart of the one they hurt. You have already hurt mine. Remember it well. I love you, Manuel, but this is a betrayal of the heart that you rocked in your arms to the rhythm of trust. You cry, but I'm dying inside. Be happy, but without me."

Ana decided to break up with Manuel because of a lie. It is difficult to understand how such a trifle could have a consequence of such magnitude, but Ana was like that; loyal to herself, strong as a rock, serene as the breeze that caresses the barley, and stubborn as a mule.

They ended their courtship in an instant. They were two broken and wandering hearts; she convinced that falsehood was reason enough to take the most painful step of her entire life; he preoccupied that his betrayal had not been such, that he actually deserved to be heard and understood. And so, the months passed, two souls without light, wandering in a sea of sorrow.

May, with its overflowing greenery, its voluptuous flowering, the smell of rockrose and heat that flushes the cheeks, was the perfect morning to go down to the river to wash. Ana got ready, and with Luz, took the wicker baskets for the laundry, the homemade soap, and the packed lunch for while the clothes were drying stretched out in the sun.

The two of them were talking about their daily chores when they turned the corner to leave Bellavista de la Jara and saw Manuel. Ana wanted to turn around, but Luz did not let her, grabbed her arm and said: "Don't even move, he must see you as haughty as a cypress".

"Good morning, Luz, good morning, Ana,"

"Good morning, Master Manuel, we can't stop too long because we are going to do the washing in the river and the others have already gone ahead," said Luz politely.

"That's okay, Luz. Ana, can I talk to you for a second?"

"If it's just a second, yes. What can I do for you?" she said, looking down her nose, disdainfully.

"Ana, I've been told that a distant cousin of yours, Juan Antonio, from Algeciras, is trying to woo you. Is that true?"

"Why should I give you any explanation? Did you give me any over your Sarita?"

"Maybe because I love you and cannot forget you, or maybe because I am dying without you, or maybe because the regret is as great as the blood that runs through my body."

"Yes, he is courting me, and my parents are very happy."

"But Ana, do you love him?"

"What's that to you? Besides, whatever decision I make, you're not in my life."

"Are you sure about that? Don't you want to give me another chance?"

"No! He who lies once will lie hundreds of times. It's better this way. I'm going, Manuel. Be happy with whoever you find to be happy with."

"Goodbye, Ana. Thank you, my life, because the love that I have felt, and that you have made me feel, I will never find again. You are my Ana forever."

"Feel what you please, I've already forgotten you."

This encounter ended in the worst of ways. Manuel left with tears of blood in his heart; broken by the pain of not winning her forgiveness; wounded by the jealousy that eats away at the soul like the worst of plagues; and without hope, now all was lost.

Ana with the birth of a river of tears that, without consolation, flowed from the deepest part of her being, without looking back, clinging to the wicker basket and sinking her hands into its corners, so that the pain she felt would be less than the emotional pain.

Both wanting to turn around and kiss each other, but neither did, they went their separate ways with their broken feelings.

Manuel did what he had to do, that which was expected of him. Before the summer arrived, he enlisted for his military service, and like his father, he went to Madrid, with the difference that he was in the Air Force in Getafe. He had two years ahead of him to think about what to do with his life and to forget Ana, if that was even possible.

Ana, on the contrary, accepted her life without Manuel, and at the insistence of her parents, she accepted being wooed by Juan Antonio. But this also had its consequences. Juan Antonio was in love with Ana to the core. He gave everything for her. He admired her serene beauty, her simplicity, her candor, her spontaneity and freshness, or in his words, "she kissed wherever she stepped". But for Ana, Juan Antonio was more like a friend, a confidant to a certain extent, and a green mulberry to remove the stain of the other purple one.

Their engagement was quickly formalized as everyone was in a hurry for it to take shape, to have an ideal outcome, and for Ana to forget Manuel once and for all.

"Ana, my queen, I have brought you a surprise from Algeciras. Come, open it."

"Juan Antonio, really, you don't have to buy me anything, it's not necessary, besides, it's not ladylike to accept gifts."

"Ana, you are my girlfriend. I can, and I want to, bring them for you. Everything I see seems too little for you. If you'd let me, I would buy you a thousand things to your liking. I would even put flowers in your bedroom."

"Juan Antonio, don't go there! There are places that are unmentionable for a decent woman!"

"Don't get angry, it was just a figure of speech."

"I know, but look what happened to me at Midnight Mass with Manuel."

"Ana, he is always on your lips. Is there nothing I do or say to you that you won't respond with his name? Sometimes, I even feel that he is sitting between us."

"Juan Antonio, don't say that. I only remembered that moment because of what you said just now."

"Ana, I love you madly. And you?"

"Why do you constantly ask me how I feel? Isn't it enough to see how happy I am in your presence? I have given you a "yes" and we are sweethearts, so let everything take shape."

"Ana, give me a kiss, on my cheek, that's all I ask."

"No, Juan Antonio, you are forcing me to do what I do not want to do."

"Ana, you are lying to me about your feelings just like Manuel lied to you. You are acting the same way, if not worse. You are trying to force yourself to love me, when you don't really feel anything. You are still in love with Manuel."

"Please, Juan Antonio, don't talk to me like that. Though it's true that I can't forget him, I'm not lying to you. I just need more time."

"I think, Ana, that our courtship has come to an end. After a year of going back and forth from Algeciras, in love with you to the hilt, I have not been able to get you to say "I love you" even once. You have lied to me, hiding your true feelings, not being able to tell me that you will never really love me like you love him. I wish you all the best and hopefully life will reward you with his true love or someone else's, but you don't love me."

"You are right, even if I tell myself that everything will change, that I will love you and that we will be happy, I always think about him. If I have lied to you, it was not consciously or with the intention of hurting you, but it is true, we should not continue to nurture what does not grow. Thank you for all your understanding and your time. I too hope that you find the love you deserve."

"If life doesn't treat you well, remember that I will always be there. And if you feel there is a chance, no matter how small, it will be enough for me."

Yes, Ana's courtship with Juan Antonio lasted a year. Neither the gifts, nor the flattery, nor the great love he had for her could drown the feelings she had for Manuel. There are loves that with the passage of time grow like a ball of incandescent fire that occupies the whole chest. Sometimes with blue tones and other times like hot lava that burns you inside making it impossible to forget that passion.

Chapter XV
The Imaginary Night

"Don't cling to the memory," Ana would say to herself, "don't dwell with the past in your heart, in your throat and in your mouth, spitting out memories that scourge your being, making you rejoice in pain. Don't say that your life only has meaning when he is here. Is it possible to forget?". Ana repeated to herself that you only forget what you have to forget, nothing more and nothing less, because what has to remain until we assimilate it, remains and endures, coming out like that latent virus, herpes, that reappears time and again in the form of cold sores. No matter what your defenses, no matter how hard you try, it stays hidden there.

There was a name, Juan Antonio, moments, years later that she was not able to remember, that remained locked in the box of oblivion. However, there was another name, Manuel, which by degrees she'd wanted to be forgotten, but which clung to her mind, making her drunk with stories that were not worthy of remembrance or with which her mind was filled with feelings of pain and victimhood. And the most curious thing is that they did not appear in a row, but sporadically, whenever an external event triggered them. Then her mind took over her heart and, if she let the words come out of her mouth, she questioned herself in such a way that she was unable to get out of the loop. But it was then that her inner warrior, brandishing the sword of love, drew strength from where there was none, so that the words would not leave her lips and would return to where they belonged, and that "I love you, Manuel" was protected again in that place where you want to drown your feelings.

"It's my birthday, November 2nd," Manuel thought, sitting in the sentry box huddled under his greatcoat. What a moon! Could they be seeing it like this in Bellavista de la Jara? A halo of nostalgia, tinted with disappointment led him to think of his town, his mother, his father and siblings; but there was a half-formed thought that he would not let emerge. Every time her face, her name or her smile came to his mind, he pushed it again and again to the side trying to get it out of his mind. But he couldn't. He kept coming back to her eyes; to that first kiss following that theatrical slap, which had satiated his senses and his soul. Would she perhaps be remembering him on this day, on his birthday? Would she think of his kisses, his stolen glances in the mass, his courage in asking to be allowed to start a formal courtship? Doubts and more doubts gnawed his insides, "what an absurd fool and imbecile I was! How could I have done something so stupid?".

The night became even more present; the moon almost over his head pinpointed him with its brightness; inquisitive, haughty and seductive. Perhaps the moon was talking to him about Ana? What nonsense one thinks in forced solitude! He had already decided to forget her, to leave her in the village so as not to feel her, see her and smell her again. She had made it quite clear to him that his lie was enough to break a real love. "I'm an idiot, why did I ever listen to Paco? Ever since he told me that Ana had broken up with Juan Antonio I do nothing but hurt myself with perverse illusions that bring me nothing but this mean loneliness".

Manuel let the night pass, but at dawn, his deep feelings and desires for Ana came pouring out; the wound opened up and he felt that he loved her more than ever. Without her it was impossible to live and so, words which were to last through the years, and from generation to generation, were written; words that he didn't have to think about, because they were simply already written.

Getafe, November 2, 1953

Dearest and beloved Ana:

I hereby wish you well and all your family. I am on duty, as you can see, on my birthday. Today is my birthday, did you remember? But whether you remembered it or not is not what leads me to pen these words to you.

Ana, my whole life, my love, my madness, my whim, my weakness, my torture. As much as I want to forget you, I can't. I'm not capable; my body and my head are on fire as penance for such a blunder, but it was a harsh punishment for such a foolish action.

Ana, forget my lie, leave it in the past and I swear I will never again tell any falsehood, whether I am with you or not.

Forgive me with my heart wide open. I will return at Christmas, and if you permit me, I want to tell you before our Blessed Virgin that my love is complete, eternal and faithful, that you will never again doubt me, and that without you I will never be happy.

As you read these heart-wrenching words it is my hope and wish that you will understand that this is the purest and most sincere statement, the fullest I could ever make. If you decide not to see me, it won't make any difference, because I will continue to love you for life. My dearest and beloved Ana, you are impossible to forget.

Always yours if you let me be,

Manuel

Manuel cried that morning. Seeing himself writing the most sincere letter of his life, disgorging everything he felt in his heart, to see himself moved -when that was a woman's thing- made him feel broken, empty, aimless and full of questions. Should he send it? Would she read it? What would she think? Would there be an answer? Was it worth wasting time thinking about such things? Of course, it was the most sensible and real thing to do because he had the hope of changing the future. Without Ana nothing made any real sense, or perhaps any sense at all.

At the end of the watch, he arrived at his barracks, took a hot shower and tucked the letter under his pillow. He had a few hours ahead of him to rest and stop dying little by little.

"Ana, come down, there's a letter from Madrid."

"From Madrid, Mother? For me?"

"Yes, daughter, it's for you. Come, I want to talk to you before you open it."

"Mother, don't worry, I'm not going back to him."

"Ana, is it possible for you to be quiet for a moment? You know, quieter, prettier. I want to tell you something. Please, listen quietly, but with your ears wide open. I have heard you cry every night for a year and a half. I have seen you try to love someone else and not succeed. I have seen you languish in front of the sewing even though you are passionate about it. I have watched you die little by little, not physically, but the death of your hope. If in the letter, Manuel is repentant, and you believe his words, and you are willing to turn the page forever, read it with all your being and trust in God's crooked paths. And before you go up to your room to read it, give me one of those big hugs you give to your father, but don't tell him."

"Mother, how much I love you!"

With her heart in her throat, excited and thrilled, she climbed the stairs two at a time, with the letter stuck to her chest, unconsciously praying to God that in that letter she might find healing for the tear-jerking sickness. She placed it at the foot of the bed, unbuttoned her black shoes and lay down. She looked for a moment at the Virgin on her bedside table, realized that there was too little light, and went to the balcony to open the shutters. Feeling cold, she decided to get into bed, and began to read.

She hugged the pillow and kissed it again and again, as if time and space were crossing to caress her Manuel's face, hang on his neck and kiss him endlessly and without limit.

"Mother, I'm so nervous. I'm finally going to see him."

"My daughter, always remember your honor and your virtue. You are going to a party at Don Juan Cruz's house, let nothing be said about the upbringing I have given you."

"Mother, please don't doubt me. My joy is like the explosion of a firework, but my values and beliefs outweigh any hopes."

"Oh, dear God, let it be what you ordain!"

Ana opened the door slowly; a slap of icy air shook her. She had not expected it to be so cold, although she should have, since the afternoon was leaden, threatening snow. She fitted her fingers, like a puzzle, into her navy-blue woolen gloves, before adjusting the belt of the cloth coat of the same color; and put on the imitation angora scarf that Aunt Irene had knitted her for Christmas Eve. She covered her mouth with it and started walking.

She caught herself humming a carol.

Let's not give the child any more strawberry trees or he will get drunk with them....

She was so happy that she could not believe it! However, a mental storm also threatened as with every step her inner voice repeated: "What if he lies to you again? He won't! He knows it would be the last time he would see me; he knows he would kill me inside; he won't". She arrived without feeling she had come a long way, despite not feeling her feet or hands; her nose was cold and red, just like her little face. She knocked and Josefina opened the door.

"Come on in, Ana, it's freezing cold."

"You don't say, I'm colder than a penguin."

"But, Ana, what's wrong with your face?"

"Nothing. Why?"

"You're blue," her friend said, laughing heartily.

"Blue? Don't tell me that. I've spent three hours getting ready and I've put on one of my sister's creams. Blue, for God's sake, Josefina, you're making me feel on edge!"

"Ana, you look like a picture and Manuel is going to swoon when he sees you like this!" The nervous laughter made her unable to disguise it.

"Ana, is that you?"

Blue! Manuel was behind her. She wanted to die of embarrassment. She didn't have time to go backwards to the bathroom.

"Yes, it's me, but I need a minute."

"Ana, turn around, I can't wait to look you in the eye."

"Yes, yes, but give me a minute."

Manuel took her by the arm and turned her around.

"Who is this Ana with the blue beard?" He smiled and, with great gentleness, he removed the remains of the angora wool from his beloved's face.

Every time his fingers touched her, shivers ran down both their spines; their gazes were glued to each other; they kissed with them; and all the while they were unable to say a single word. Why, this time there was no need to say, "I love you".

Music could be heard in the adjoining room, a living room decorated with carpets and mirrors and a huge fireplace that presided over the back wall. They entered slowly, Ana clutching Manuel's arm, and suddenly, all their friends cheered and hugged the couple, because it was time for their reconciliation and to be cured of the ailment of tears.

"Ana, are you aware of how much I love you?"

"Manuel, are you aware of all that I have suffered?"

"Ana, we have both suffered. I have tried everything to forget you; I have tried to fall in love with nice girls; I have gone out dancing or taken them for ice cream, but it always ended with the same story: "you, you, and a thousand times you". But it won't happen again, I am a man, and you will be my Ana, my dear and beloved Ana, this time forever.

They were at Don Juan Cruz's door, in the hallway. Manuel could wait no longer, between one cloying phrase and another, not knowing what else to say, he approached her mouth, that mouth he dreamed of day and night, and let himself go. Ana accepted longingly, tired of so many words. They came together in such a way that the expected innocent kiss became the most ardent kiss they had ever given each other.

The heat of their mouths and the humidity of an incipient desire hit their bodies; desiring and loving each other, a madness of feelings stirred their insides in that unique and unrepeatable kiss. Ana remembered her mother's words about her virtue, but she didn't have to stop that kiss. Manuel was so nervous that his legs and his whole body trembled.

He took a step back and inadvertently nudged the huge vase to the left of the door. They suddenly separated being aware of the feverish, ardent and generous love in their hearts and bodies.

She wanted a kiss like that; don't we all? She wanted to melt; she wanted to tremble; she wanted to shake her heart and turn it inside out like a sock; she didn't care if her legs gave way and she fell on her ass; she wanted to look like a fool -if that meant she was cured of the weeping sickness- she wanted to live "the now" in a kiss that enveloped the most beautiful gift, the silly smile of a lover who was not afraid to dance to the beat of another heart.

Chapter XVI
What if I marry the father and you marry the son?

"Sew, Ana. You're scatterbrained. You're pricking yourself without realizing it. You've already got three pricks on your middle finger. Maybe it's just because you're in love and a little crazy."

Maria was sewing next to her, next to the window with wooden shutters. They were sewing little girl's dresses. Ana gathered all her wits to learn quickly. She had to do it as she would soon be going to the capital to learn dressmaking. She could not make a fool of herself; her self-esteem forced her to seek perfection in her actions as if her life depended on it; "asserting herself" in everything.

"Ana, what are you thinking? You've been stitching and un-stitching all afternoon. You're stitching clumsily as if you're in a daze."

"Me? Yes, maybe. Manuel arrives tomorrow on leave, and I'm shaken up inside. I can't eat or sleep; I can't concentrate, and everything seems to me to be happening at a dinosaur's pace."

"You're in love! That's good. Don't think that all that feeling is just giddiness, rather, you are growing inside."

"Maria, have you ever been in love?"

"That's not something to tell a brat like you, but maybe I'll tell you a secret."

"Come clean, I'm all ears."

"No, no, little girl. Don't ever tell anything you don't want to be known; never say it, because feelings are a silver powder, which in someone else's mouth becomes the cannon fodder of gossip."

"Don't keep me in suspense. I can keep a secret."

"Yes, Ana, but it could be that in a slip of the tongue you tell your mother, who tells your aunts, and from there it's all over the market...."

"Well, as you like. But you can trust me. Besides, honestly, I know what you're going to tell me."

"Crazy, that's what I think you are." Both burst out laughing.

"What if I marry the father and you marry the son?"

Manuel arrived early in the morning in a truck that had brought him from the Bailen crossroads. He was tired, but he wanted the day to start so he could send a message to Ana and capture her with his eyes. He gave two loud raps with the knocker and the locks inside sounded as if they were opening the gates of paradise. He was home at last. He embraced his father, Samuel, and then sat down in front of the fire and recounted all the escapades he'd been involved in since the beginning of the year.

After enjoying a fragrant and comforting percolated coffee, Manuel had a good bath, shaved, put on civilian clothes, his clean shoes and cologne, a special water that his father used, one with a fresh smell.

"Manuel, saddle up my mare, I want to go with you to the pasture."

"But, father, I want to see Ana."

"You'll have time later. Now I want you to come with me. We have things to talk about. They are not trifles and the important things are said better sooner rather than later."

"As you wish, father."

Somewhat annoyed, he prepared his father's mare, put on espadrilles and when everything was ready, went in search of him. It was early, but there was still that freshness of June mornings, when the sun is not yet strong, but the clouds announce a hot day. With difficulty, yet with dexterity, Samuel climbed on Licenciada, adjusted his feet in the stirrups and took the reins.

They did not speak, Manuel had no idea what his father was going to tell him, but it certainly must be important. Breaking that heavy silence was complicated as daring to disfigure it with a trifle could incite his father's anger, or at the very least, bewilderment. It was better to remain silent. Samuel, on the other hand, was looking for the right words to let his firstborn know the decisions that had already been made.

"Manuel, I am going to tell you something and I am not asking your opinion, because what I am going to tell you is a decision that has already been made. It is for the sake of your sisters, for the good of the house and for my own sake." Again, a dense silence enveloped them, the minutes did not seem to pass, but both could recognize the time elapsed between the inhalation and exhalation of each one.

"Father, I need to know what the hell is going on!" He grabbed Licenciada's reins bringing him to a halt.

"Manuel, I am going to marry Maria. She is a good woman. She has served us at home for a long time. She is a very honest woman, reserved, industrious, who knows how to economize and run a house. Besides, your sisters love her very much."

"Father, that's not a bad thing. But you already have a grandmother and an aunt living with you, I don't think you need to marry."

"I don't want your opinion. As I have already told you, I just want to let you to know the decision I have made. I want you to be aware that Maria is a virgin, she never had any contact with any man that I know of, and I must make her a woman and a mother.

"Are you crazy, father? Are you telling me you want to have another child when you already have four? You've forgotten mother, haven't you? It is clear that what you are looking for is selfish; a woman to take care of you and satisfy your virile needs. Enough of this nonsense! I can't believe that I am hearing such idiocy from you. You have let me down, father." he said, turning away from the horse and his father.

"I am not going to allow you to disrespect me. I am going to marry Maria and I am going to give her a child, or as many as come. She is going to be the lady of the house and your grandmother, and your aunt will go home. Life is going to change whether you like it or not. I only expect you to rise to the occasion as the eldest son. I hope that I never hear that you have spoken of this conversation. Do not even think of mentioning or discussing it in the plazas or casinos. Respect all of us, at all times, and remember who your father is. And if you don't like it, tough luck. You know where you can go; although I'll wish with all my heart that it were not so, for it will be on your conscience. Now go back to town and go wherever you have to go, but keep your mouth shut about family matters or face the consequences. Goodbye, Manuel, go with God."

Manuel looked at Samuel through very different lenses. The state of mind, their own needs, the selfishness they dragged along, were ingredients impossible to objectify, acting as prisms with an infinite rainbow of possibilities that unquestionably nuanced the perception of facts and feelings.

So, was it not possible for Manuel to see it the way his father did? Yes, it was possible, but the task was of such magnitude that it could not be done lightly, nor could the importance it had for him be ignored. He wanted to put himself in his father's shoes in order to understand, without losing his mind, or leaving behind what he thought about his father marrying again. But he had to listen to what his father was telling him; to analyze what his father felt in his conscience to make such a categorical change in his own life. If he could not forget his mother, Angela, how could his father wish to marry again? Just imagining the situation, contemplating it and then living it, already hurt his soul. He was aware that no one made decisions just for the sake of it, especially not when the consequences of his decisions would affect other people like his own children.

But at that instant he thought of Ana, saying to himself, "Do not judge me when I tell you my concerns, Ana, as I am doing with my father. Don't judge my changes of decision; don't make gestures at me when you do not understand my reactions, or when they seem crazy to you; don't think negatively about me when you do not agree; don't accuse me of being an unthinking madman when my intuition leads me to say black or white; rather, analyze with me why I feel that way; why I've decided such a thing; why I can't for the life of me; or why I am simply happy. If we do this, it will be fully evident that we respect each other and that love is above all else".

Manuel did not allow himself to understand his father, for fear of being judged, analyzed, ousted from his full conviction that the memory of his mother was above all, and the best for everyone. In any case, respect for a father, for what he represents and, in a certain way, having observed the reality of the situation, made the decision taken plausible and correct. But it is another thing to accept love from a woman other than one's own mother; to accept having more siblings, when one is already over eighteen and, logically, one should think more about having children than new siblings. Although it was something that Manuel could not imagine, he could only assert, that, from that conjugal love, with the passage of time, would be born his sister, Raquel, beautiful and intelligent, lively and special, whom Manuel has always loved with all his heart.

Chapter XVII
Decide for me

When you live what you desire, no matter how it happened, it is truly incomprehensible and heartwarming. But what does it take to make the things we wish to live happen? That is the chimera and the magic of life, the unknown future coupled with longed-for desires. And suddenly, when you least expect it, a chain of events causes your life to change and in what a way! Blessed causality!

Sara, September 20, 2018.

Ana let the days go by waiting for Manuel's letter, and on Saturdays she had a long-distance call on the telephone, although these conversations always left her sad. She deliberately left the most important things unsaid; sometimes so as not to worry Manuel; other times for not being heard by her relations that were operators, who always "unintentionally" left some cord plugged in, only to later go with the story to her mother; sometimes because her hormones got out of balance and made her angry for not hearing from her beloved the words she wanted so much; but whichever it was, Saturdays dawned with the hope of hearing his voice and ended with a bittersweet taste.

At the age of twenty-three, incredibly, she was already an old maid, according to the malicious tongues, who said that Manuel, with time and being alone in Madrid, would meet a lady who would steal his love, or would give him the gift of her daily presence. She embroidered her trousseau with delicacy and with a certain disdain because she didn't know when the moment would come for it to be laid out. Sometimes, in her full youth, she felt old to undertake a life of love; she thought that her soul was losing its joy; she only prayed for the joy of being with him. At night, she felt lonely, she cried silently "hold me and make me understand that you will not leave, that you will look after me for a lifetime". Really, all their courtship had developed at a distance with few moments of confidences; perpetual conversations in which to imagine plans in common; infinite glances in search of the "us". But she also realized that he was everything to her; the strength of her life; the essence that only with a letter was dispersed throughout her being. So, it was on her lips she carried a thousand "I love yous" forever and ever.

In those anguishes covered with smiles to her own, she clung to God, her faithful friend. She made her most intimate confidences to him, even promising herself that if Manuel did not crystalize her love, she would go into a convent. She could never be loved by another man, desired by other eyes, she was his and for him alone. It was the story of an eternal love engraved in every pore of her skin; to detach herself from that love would be to strip off her skin. From that first time that his gray eyes pierced her, she understood that her Manuel was the reason for her life; she was unable to stop loving him, no matter what it cost her.

That afternoon in March 1959, the eve of her birthday, she was choking at home, the air was thick in her room and the specks of dust suspended in the rays coming through the window were even thicker than at other times. She didn't feel like sewing or reading; she didn't want to talk to her sisters. She went out into the courtyard in search of the warmth of the sun, but even its heat made her uncomfortable. She entertained herself by putting water on her father's partridges, watered the flower in their pots, wet her forehead to try to cool her thoughts; she even took off her shoes to wet her little feet and feel the coolness of the water, and ended up sitting on the small stairs that served as the access to the back rooms. Without realizing it, she noticed how tears welled up in her eyes and ran down her pretty face. It was melancholy, nostalgia, unhappiness, sadness.... She did not know how to diagnose her state of mind, she was only certain that she was not happy.

Her mother unexpectedly entered the courtyard, and with a glance questioned why she was crying, to which Ana responded with anguish and a cry that came from the deepest part of her heart. They both looked at each other in silence, her mother knew perfectly well the illness Ana was suffering from, and if she opened her mouth she would hurt her much more, because what she was provoked to tell her was a list of arguments that discredited Manuel's love because he had not taken the step of marrying her daughter. It was better to remain silent, not to make the heart of her little girl bleed more. She decided to give her a kiss on the cheek, wiping the wetness from her little face with her hands and returned to the kitchen. Ana stayed a while longer, while she calmed her mind, and maybe even her heart. And she decided to go inside to ask her mother's permission to walk in the square.

She tied her hair, soaped her hands and face, gave a big sigh and tied her shoes, put a little gloss on her lips and clicked her tongue in a "what can we do, life goes on". She left without saying goodbye, but Fatima, watched her from behind the window as she walked away up the hill. She noticed the languor of her posture and her slack, almost lazy shuffling gait, and her characteristic slight limp that so saddened her heart ever since her little girl, then just two years old, had suffered polio. She drew the curtain and prayed all the short prayers known to her to ask God to not let her Ana suffer.

"Ana, wait a moment."

"Samuel, how are you? What can I do for you?"

"Where are you going, Ana? You look sad, has something happened that I don't know about?"

"What do you mean, Samuel? I'm all right. It's just a bad day, I guess."

"Ana, I would like you to count on me for everything and, of course, if something happens, I can help you."

"Don't worry about me, Samuel, everything is fine," she said, looking away to hide the tears that were about to flow from her eyes, and wanting to scream at him that she couldn't stand his son Manuel, anymore; that she didn't know what was going to become of her life; that the years were passing; that she was already an adult; that she was even a little old maid to the wagging tongues.

"Ana, look at me."

"Samuel, for God's sake, I'm having a bad day. I just feel like crying. Don't worry, really. I'm going for a walk and it will pass. I'll go to see the Virgin. I'm sure she'll take away the nonsense I'm carrying inside."

"Ana, it's because of my son, isn't it? You're tired of waiting."

"Don't... you say that," she sobbed.

"Ana, my daughter, do you really love him?"

"Of course! I love him truly, with all my soul. I am dying thinking that he will not come back or that he will fall in love with someone else. The "spinsters" tell me that he will fall in love with another woman in Madrid and that he will forget me and that all my time will have been buried in a broken youth. But

Samuel, I know that your son loves me, otherwise, why have I suffered so much pain."

"I want to talk to you very seriously. Take my handkerchief and wipe away those tears, which make you look like a little girl. Let's go sit on that bench in the square. I'm sure that the coolness of the fountain will reach us from there and we'll appreciate it because this March is almost like May. You're calmer now, aren't you?"

She nodded her assent, head bowed.

"I am going to talk to you as I would talk to one of my daughters, so I want you to pay close attention to me. Once I tell you what I think, you will tell me from the bottom of your heart whether I am right or wrong. Do you agree?"

"Yes, Samuel, I will answer you from my heart and with the whole truth."

"Ana, you have told me that you love my son Manuel with all your heart, and I know that he loves you deeply too. I also know that my son is not able to get the savings he needs to take the leap you are hoping for, to buy a house and get married. After finishing the militia and becoming a clerk at the hotel, he has very little money. Do you understand, Ana? Well, here's the question: do you want to marry my son, Manuel?"

"Don Samuel! You can't ask me something that your son must do. You can't ask me in his name to marry him. Have you talked about it? I'm going out of my mind. You can't make me such a proposal."

"Stop it, Ana. Like all women, you're becoming overwrought. My son doesn't know anything about this, but as a father, it's time to take action. You've loved each other since you were kids, letting time go by without helping my son puts him in a dangerous situation that could cause him to lose his happiness and, Ana, my daughter, I won't allow that. But answer me: Do you want to marry my son, Manuel?"

"Yes, I do! I absolutely do. I have never wanted anything else in my life. Yes, and a thousand times yes, even if I am telling you, his father, with all due respect, of course," she said crying and smiling with eyes shining with happiness.

"Tomorrow I'm going to talk to your father. I'm going to sell a property and I'm going to give you the down payment for an apartment, and in exchange, you'll set the date of your wedding. Is that a deal, Ana? Go on, give me one of those real hugs and then run home and tell your mother about it. Later I'll look for your father, since I already have a buyer. I'm looking forward to going to a wedding... and having grandchildren" he laughed.

Ana was excited, no matter the how, the important thing was to achieve the goals. She had achieved it when she least expected it, when the sadness was overwhelming her, in the most unusual way, but she got her marriage proposal. Not from the son, but from the father.

She was immensely happy with the proposal of the father of her fiancé; she did not need the confirmation of a ring, or a dinner, or with flowers. It was with simplicity and the purest love towards his children that led Samuel to take the step on behalf of his son, albeit without his knowledge, much less consent; but he knew he had made the right decision, because it would accelerate the happiness of his son and Ana.

He was aware of what loneliness in Madrid entailed for Manuel, and what might happen if his son did not have the woman he loved by his side.

Chapter XVIII
"I do" means for a lifetime

"How I do love you, Manuel," said Ana sitting on a rock at the Los Órganos lookout point. Can you explain to me why you have been so serious during the whole wedding and celebration?" she said, looking at the ground with glassy eyes.

"Ana, so many people; so many kisses; so many 'you have to take care of her, she is now under your protection'; so many 'you cannot fail us'; so many 'you must work even harder to take care of and raise the children to come'! But Ana, the most important question for me is: 'will I know how to make you happy?'"

"I just told you that I love you, Manuel. I have been happy ever since I knew I was in love with you. Let the world go hang, and trust in us and in God."

The arrival at her home was entirely enigmatic as Ana did not really know where she was going to live. It is true that she knew the address, what she would find near her home, but she was never asked to participate in the simple decoration of her small palace; her parents and her in-laws, together with Manuel, had done everything. Why? That is the most radical and bizarre question. No more and no less than for "virtue": she could not remain alone with her beloved Manuel, that being little more than frivolous and perfidious according to the morals of the time and the closed and marmoreal decency of her mother.

Suddenly the door to her home opened, a tiny entrance painted in a Versace red that blinded her eyes and furniture with rounded black and white lines. Like *Alice in Wonderland*, she crept in almost on tiptoe, fearing she would brush against something and what her eyes were seeing would vanish. When she reached her tiny kitchen with the little terrace that would serve to store everything she wanted and a small sink where she would wash with love and care her Manuel's clothes, she did not know whether to cry, laugh, jump, or scream. It did not matter what she did because at that moment, Manuel took her by the waist, poured all the tenderness in the world on her lips, all the love that her body and her heart allowed her. Ana, with her heart about to explode and her body like a volcano, responded to his warm kiss with more kisses, letting her body feel, feel and feel for the first time more than she had ever imagined. Manuel grabbed her hand, they were wet from the nerves that gripped them both, he squeezed it tightly to which Ana responded with an affectionate "ow". They arrived at the door of the double bedroom, where Ana stopped in her tracks. She froze. She suddenly realized that she was going to give herself to Manuel and she knew nothing more than four little details that her older sister had told her. She suddenly wanted to leave, to run, to get lost, she was panicked, afraid, dreadful, suspicious and even a little apprehensive.

"Ana, come."

"No, I can't."

"Ana, my life, don't be afraid, nothing will happen that we don't both want. I love you with all my soul. I would never do anything that you wouldn't want, nothing that would hurt you, nothing that I would regret. If you are not ready, I will just sleep in the embrace of my beautiful wife.

Ana smiled slightly and, giving him her hand, crossed the threshold of that room of a thousand and one dreams. Manuel looked deeply into her eyes, gently caressed the nape of her neck and slid his fingers along her small left earlobe. He moved down to her back delicately and approached her trembling lips, a subtle touch gave way to the warm friction of their mouths, she did not know how to behave, nor what she should do, she was not even aware that she had to do anything.

"Do you love me, Ana?" asked Manuel with eyes full of desire and love.

"Why do you ask me that?"

"Because you are rigid; you don't move; you don't blink; you don't even sigh."

"I don't know what to do," she said, starting to cry, "I'm nervous and embarrassed."

"Ana, this is not a sin. It is just loving each other. Caressing you and kissing you must be something that you also desire and do in the same way with me."

"Manuel, I don't know how to act."

"Ana, you don't have to act, just love. Come here and give me a hug, you must relax and so must I. Maybe it's better if we cuddle in bed and tomorrow will be another day. Don't grieve, my life, you don't know what love is, except in your imagination and, of course, you have no idea how to animate it. I love you, my life, nothing will happen. Come and snuggle on my chest and sleep."

As expected, after Manuel's understanding, both began the most delicate and passionate act of love, shame, taboos, sin... were left behind as they became a single being.

Chapter XIX
And you were a mother

On January 10, 1961, her firstborn, Ignacio, was born; a baby who was almost born at ten months according to Ana. It could be considered more or less, the birth of a donkey: ugly and lanky, the opposite of what Ignacio is now. His mother's first love. She was all heart, as she taught him to be, all love and all faith. And on January 29, 1963, Luis was born: a gorgeous, chubby baby with huge olive-green eyes, and cuddly as could be.

After a few years of happy marriage, of Manuel's moonlighting, of sewing clothes for them at night, of cleaning and cooking at dawn, Christmas 1964 arrived. Ana and Manuel together with their children traveled to Bellavista de la Jara. Their arrival was as usual: Ana going to her parents' house with the children, Manuel to see his father and family, where he made plans with the others without taking into account that Ana was left with the rest of the obligations. This scene, reiterated in every trip to Bellavista de la Jara, produced a wave of gossip in both families, and outside of them, which made Ana arrive predisposed to cut through the tittle tattle, whether at the table or with Manuel's laissez-faire attitude. She never liked to be the subject of gossip, much less abandoned by the one she loved most in this world.

Manuel arrived at his in-laws' house after lunchtime. Ana, sitting in the rocking chair, was rocking Luis to sleep in her arms, an arduous and complicated task because the motion of the rocking chair in question was more like a roller coaster than a loving "go to sleep my child". Manuel, unwary, reached over to give Ana a kiss on the cheek. She pulled her face away and looked at him with "if you say the slightest thing to me, I'll scratch you" eyes, but Manuel, in a sardonic voice, asked her if he could have something to eat.

The scene, so common in all couples, is repeated from generation to generation. Women who stay with their children and obligations and men who make their freedom of movement a bastion, a flagship of their masculinity which cannot be disrupted during their vacation periods.

Ana remained with her eyes fixed on Manuel, rocking and rocking, harder and harder, until the rocking chair in question hit the wall, then she got up, handed little Luis to his father and went to the kitchen.

"He's all yours," she said. "People are making comments about me and your children, about us. Don't forget they are your children too."

Manuel suddenly lost any hint of the joyous exaltation that comes from sherry and good cheese. Undaunted, he questioned her with his eyes, waited a few seconds and, having no answer, left for his father Samuel's house.

The afternoon languished quickly into an early evening. Each time her mother stirred the brazier to make the heat more intense, it burnt her shins and the coal dust made Ana's head dizzy. She did not speak except to correct Ignacio or make to croons to Luis. Night came and Manuel did not appear, but the first questions from her mother and the expected reproaches did.

"I told you. Manuel is smart. As always when he comes here, he comes first, he comes second, and his family comes third. Who knows who he hangs out with and what he's saying."

Ana began to worry. She fed the little ones their dinner and put them to bed. The next day was Christmas Eve. They could not live like this, but she was not going to give up either. He had to mature, realize that his children and she came first. He had made mistakes that had caused her anger; indeed, he had defended the words of third parties that had really offended Ana.

"It's okay if he doesn't come with me, he'll be better off without me," Ana said to herself.

It was snowing at dawn. She smelled freshly brewed coffee and *tortitas* -a candy similar to pancakes but crunchy and fried in olive oil-, but Ana felt only anguish when she touched Manuel's side of the bed; it was cold and unslept in. She got up with a pain in her chest that she had not felt for years, it was the pain of the tear-sickness that she knew so well. She went downstairs after her ablutions, grooming her hair and dressing Ignacio and Luis. She went into the kitchen and there was her mother.

"Good morning, Ana, you must have slept soundly knowing that your Manuel hasn't set foot here."

"Good morning, mother. Well, no, I haven't slept, and I'd be grateful if you wouldn't take sides, as you, and Manuel's family gossips, have already talked enough."

"Are you calling me a gossip?"

"No, Mother. I'm telling you to stop repeating everything; that flies can't enter a closed mouth; that I'm quite unwell and that I want to think in peace, even alone if possible."

"It seems that Madrid has raised your spirits a little bit, but remember that you are from here as much as the rest of us."

"Mother, I'm going to the market, no one will be there this early. Please look after the children."

Damn the hour he left! There were the official mourners at funerals, weepers at weddings, and gossips, whose delight was marital entanglements, at the very door of the market.

"Good morning, Ana. How well you look since you've been away. By the way, yesterday we saw Manuel singing Christmas carols from house to house, like a little boy. He must have given you the night because he was dressed in scarlet and gold."

"Good morning. You know, as soon as you return to the village you become like everyone else. I'm in a bit of a hurry, my children are up and with the work still to be done, I can't delay."

"Yes, yes, hurry up, today is Christmas Eve and tomorrow, Christmas."

She gritted her teeth for not telling them frankly what those harpies and that idiot Manuel deserved. It was enough for him, celebrating his unseemly deed. Every step she took, the more her anger and bile rose in her throat. She wanted to calm down, but it was impossible. If it had been tenable, she would have opened her mouth and let out all the poison that invaded her inside. But she was incapable. What she felt was pity. She bought what her mother had ordered and then stopped at the churro shop. Ignacio was crazy about churros, so the finicky child would eat something, although with a churro it would only be enough for half a day.

She closed her eyes, breathed the air mixed with the smoke from the oil, touched her forehead and covered her throat with the scarf, when Luz appeared.

"But, girl, how beautiful you look! Give me a cuddle. I haven't seen you for at least a year."

"Hello, Luz," said Ana, hugging her intensely and starting to cry.

"But, Ana, my girl, you look like a flooding river. What's wrong with you. Everyone can see you crying here. Come on, let's go to your aunt Irene's backyard."

Luz listened attentively to the story of what had happened, understanding what she could, because every other word was interrupted by moans and sobs. Nonetheless she got a very clear idea of what was going on. On the one hand, the helplessness that Manuel caused her when he came to town and, on the other hand, the malicious tongues that caused the confrontation between the two.

"I'm not having it. It's Christmas Eve, you have to talk to Manuel, we have to fix it."

"Even though he hasn't even come to sleep?"

"I am going to give him a message, that today at twelve o'clock he should go up to Santa Maria, where you will be waiting for him in front of the Virgin. Entrust yourself to her. But listen to me, you and your children are the most important thing. If he lets himself be manipulated by whoever, if he is not capable of helping you, if his selfishness is above all, better sooner than later. That is, it is better to be alone than in bad company. You may be tiny, but you have more mettle than that horse. Now stop crying, or you'll empty the pitcher of your little soul."

"Thank you, Luz, I don't know how to thank you for all this."

"I do. By being sincere and having the strength to defend yourself and your children. To get what you deserve, not the petty things of a playboy, who you will love madly, but who sometimes needs reminding... in short... that you are Ana and not Angela, you are not his mother."

At twelve o'clock sharp, Ana was at the door of Santa Maria with her children. As it was windy outside, she went in, Ignacio holding her little hand and Luis wrapped in his shawl, approached the lampstand and lit a candle, sat down on the first bench and waited. But Manuel did not arrive. She prayed the rosary, but he still did not appear. So, she tucked in the little one and buttoned up the older one's coat, put on her scarf and was just getting ready to leave when she heard some unmistakable footsteps, those of her Manuel.

"Have you come?" she said, looking at the ground.

"You sent me a message. Luz was very clear, either you go or you don't. What are the kids doing here?" he asked in a contemptuous tone.

"What they should, they are with their mother. They won't understand, but what I have to tell you also concerns them," she said, scowling and furious.

"Well, it's quiet here and there's no mother behind the door, so shoot."

"Don't go down that road. I have bitumen for your sins too! The problem is you arrive in town and you forget that I exist. You don't ask what I may want, what I need or if I require you to be by my side. You never stop working. I'm alone all day. I walk here, there and everywhere to the market at Ventas, sewing in the evenings, saving as much as I can. I wait for you with lunch and dinner every day, so that you won't feel the children are alienating you from me, and, even so, I am happy because that is what I have chosen my life to be. But I didn't choose to be criticized, abandoned, or play second fiddle to your whims. If you really love me, forget everything and treat me as I deserve. If not, in front of the Virgin Mary herself I swear to you that it is the end, I will get ahead with or without you."

"But, Ana, for God's sake, I don't think it's that bad."

"Manuel, either we are the most important thing in your life, or your existence is far away from us. I will not accept either my mother or anyone else questioning whether we really love each other; if we have a good marriage; if we give them their place, or whatever. You and my children are my life, first and foremost, and if we are not the same for you, you must behave like a man and tell me so."

"I beg your pardon, Ana. It's true, I have really neglected you between some things and others. I do not realize, or maybe I do, everything you do, because I take it for granted, as if you had made no sacrifice, but you are immense. You have the courage to face life no holds barred, without crutches, without letting anyone move you from the path you choose. It is true that I have to grow up. Ana, don't ever leave me, please. Without you I know how much life hurts, forgive me."

"Here, take Luis and kiss me here in front of the Virgin, because I am not one who doesn't know how to forgive you; and that is what love is, to forgive and continue walking together."

How life hurts! Yes, life sometimes hurts so much that it blinds all the senses; life sometimes hurts so much that it empties the guts and veins of life itself.

It takes you to the abyss, gives you the push you need to abandon yourself to the feeling of not drowning, even though you are short of breath, that nameless sadness that we all call "anxiety and depression".

Chapter XX
The day I was born and died through you

It is time to reveal that, through these writings, I made myself present in the past, which then I made a part of myself. I am Sara, daughter of Ana and granddaughter of Angela, third generation of a lineage of women who feel with heart.

"Sara, daughter, listen to me. It's confession night and I want you to know why you are in this blessed world, but first give me a massage here, my life, the lump is tugging my neck. I am restless and I can't quell the pain or the earthquake that runs through me."

"Shall I call a nurse? Maybe they can calm that uneasiness that is driving you to despair. Anyway, I'm going to ask for a lime tea for you, as concoctions scare you," she said smiling sweetly and walking out the door of the hospital room.

The short, shabby corridor I walked to the duty nurse's desk seemed like an unsightly route. I wondered why hospitals kept those faded, dull floors and the smell of sickness and medicines with disinfectant, together with the stench of humanity that characterizes patients and companions with long hospital stays. An irrepressible disgust rose in my throat like vomit. I breathed and discarded that thought in search of meeting the need of Ana, my mother. With the lime tea burning my fingers and a paracetamol, I returned to Room 205, wishing to resume that conversation whose content had made me the promise of knowing why am I in this blessed world?

"Mom, I'm here with your lime tea and a paracetamol. When you take it, make me a little space on your bedside and tell me what you want to tell me.

"Well, if you really want it, here it is."

September 5, 1971, having just arrived home after a beautiful vacation in Mallorca, Ana was going through the contents of the suitcases that she had meticulously laid out on the bed. The contents had come clean from the ship's laundry, but no, oh no, those machines didn't wash as conscientiously as she did! She selected the most delicate to soap first. Thus, the day went by, without stopping, but with an idea that she had brought from the vacation which, like a woodpecker, hammered her delicate thoughts.

She wondered how she should approach the fact that she wanted to be a mother again. That she knew and sensed, in that way that only women sense, that if that night she used marriage with all the love she was capable of, the consequence would be her baby girl. Manuel was going to flatly refuse. She was aware that, having lost her third premature daughter in the incubator and having had an abortion that had almost killed her, that is what would happen. She called her sister and asked her to take the children which she did and with all the joy in the world they set off for their cousins' house.

She sat quietly in front of the mirror, brushed her French-girl, brown hair and began that precious, almost liturgical ritual, in which a woman begins to transform herself as if in a chrysalis, in search of love, of the only sublime beauty, the one that comes out of the most perfect illusion of her heart. She gently applied moisturizer, a little blusher, a spark of mascara on her lively eyes and a soft layer of lipstick that she lightly dabbed on her small mouth. She tied up her hair again and looked for the bottle-green dress that favored her so much, put it on and sprayed her neck, wrists and chest with the jasmine perfume that her Manuel had given her for Christmas. And it was unintentionally, almost by chance, that the doorbell rang just then. Startled and with an excited heart, she left the room to meet Manuel. She realized that the love she had felt was so immense that the air ached, it was her drink of life, she was like a little fish, and she would always swim in its current.

Ana, with those eyes behind which lay an unmentionable secret, stood in front of Manuel and whispered: "My beloved Manuel". He, presuming that there must be more to the situation than he understood, watched her carefully. After some hesitation he asked her if something was happening and where the children were. She, lowering her eyes, responded,

"They are at my sister's house because I want to be alone with you. It's been five years since we had a moment to ourselves, where we could meet again and talk about our fortunes; about how we live and feel; about those problems that affect us and never leave us."

"What problems never leave us?"

"Things that are not relevant now," she said mischievously, winking.

"Ana, you look beautiful, my queen."

"No. Maybe just a little bit."

"You are beautiful, your eyes, your hair, your mouth, oh, my Ana!" And he hugged her.

"Come on in. Go change but don't go into the living room."

Manuel, with one of those naughty smiles, rushed to the bedroom, looked for the white shirt that Ana had put out with his suit and the freshly ironed pants. Just like his beloved Ana, he groomed himself, perfumed himself and thought: "Today the night will be eternal, my precious girl knows that I want her, I adore her, I need her. Every time I dig into the memory of the last pregnancy, my body curses itself. No, I will never get her pregnant again. Her life for me is my life itself, but seeing how she nearly bled to death, her clothes soaked, blood running down her legs, blood clots, her face white as snow and her eyes looking at me full of fear... I will never again fill her with my being, to pour myself into that immaculate body for my heart that I love more than my own children, who will not be, who are not my life! If I go against my faith, then I'll be damned; if I have to go to confession every week, I will, but I will not pour myself into my beloved Ana ever again."

"Manuel, come on, you have to open the wine I bought at the Ventas market."

"Wine? Now I'm sure you're up to something."

Ana had decorated the living room with the best from her bottom drawer: the white linen tablecloth with its hemstitches; the Christmas glassware and crockery; red carnations; and the napkins in the shape of a fan to give it that touch of her Andalusia. When Manuel had arrived home, she felt desire between her legs, the heat of her being, the rapture of the immense passion that comes from the most intense ardor of the female who wants to be a mother. Manuel sensed and glimpsed that magnetism emanating from Ana's body. He wanted to pounce on her and possess her without asking permission, without opening the wine, to fill her to the viscera with the deepest and most ardent love. But he stopped, terrified before the paralyzing idea of making her pregnant.

"Ana, when is your period due?"

"In about a fortnight, so there is no problem to make use of the marriage bed. Today is a special night."

"Are you sure? I can't do the math."

"Do you trust me? Come and kiss me properly. You look like one of those eunuchs that appear in the plays they show on television."

"If I catch you, you'll find out what's what," he said, drawing closer to her body and looking at her intently.

The dinner seasoned with kisses, playing footsie, of hands dropping on each other, made the magic of almost uncontained passion envelop them both. And so, between desperate caresses, they went to the sacred place of their love, and, in the dance of the most perfect encounter, they abandoned themselves to each other. Manuel, after giving his beloved a thousand caresses, melted into her being, and she, happy for what she had achieved, embraced him so intensely that it provoked the opposite effect, Manuel impulsively pulled away because he knew at that instant what she intended.

"Let me go, Ana."

"Please forgive me, I want another child, because I know, unequivocally, that everything will be all right. I will take care of myself and my mother will come. I swear nothing will happen this time, we will have our child, although we couldn't keep the other one through, she will be the apple of our eye and you will be crazy for her smile. Don't blame me for being alive and intuiting that this is the night when our little girl will begin to exist."

Manuel surrendered. It was done, the sentence had been delivered. The amazing fecundity of his beloved Ana meant that there was nothing he could do, and so, crestfallen, but full of love, he snuggled into her body, kissing her shoulders and surrendered to sleep.

That's how Ana told it me; how she decided, against all odds, to bring a daughter into the world, despite being aware of the potential risks. And on that last night, Ana decided to tell me more about me.

The pregnancy kept her almost incapacitated as the slightest effort made her sick and the insistent nausea made the toilet bowl her best friend. The days passed slowly in the restlessness of wanting to see the face of her little girl. She could not find the inner peace that would make her understand and admit that there was a serious risk, because her heart rejected such a possibility. And so, at seven months, a heavy bleeding occurred, the panic accompanied by the generous fear of trading her death over the life of her daughter led her to enter the hospital with her rosary clutched in her right hand, like an open verdict that she only wished would end.

After the agonizing hours of waiting without news, Manuel banged his head against the wall, causing a strong pain in his forehead, which was in no way comparable to the suffering of losing her. He cursed himself for having succumbed to her charms, disowned that damn night, and even felt a certain hateful rejection for the girl she carried in her womb, vowing, "if my Ana dies for you, I will curse you all the days of my life".

After a long time imprisoned in his inner struggle, the doctor came and released him from his hell: mother and daughter were both doing well. But as is almost always the case, after good news comes a serious situation, an intractable problem. Ana was refusing to let them take her daughter to the incubator. Her little Inmaculada, born five years earlier through an oversight or imponderable fate, fell asleep forever in that little box. She remembered with acid tears the stinging of the milk flowing from her breasts soaking her soul when she knew that tiny little girl was gone forever. Attached like an infinite and perennial umbilical cord, Ana would not let go of her daughter. The retinue of hospital staff, berating Manuel for Ana's attitude, led to Manuel himself, dressed like an actor in that gown, bursting into the recovery room to talk some sense into his beloved but stubborn Ana. Finally, he succeeded in getting the little neonate a one-night stay, at least, in that five-star hotel, the incubator.

In a few days, when Ana had recovered and her little Sara was in good shape, he requested, no, demanded, that he take his daughter home under his responsibility. He did not care if he signed a death sentence, the important thing was not to leave a daughter behind again. And I don't know how they allowed him to do so, not without first giving him specific recommendations on how to care for his little girl.

"Sara, my daughter, you could not suckle, nor did you have the strength to sneeze. You were a tiny helpless being and I took on the duty of bringing you up. Since you couldn't suck, I opened your little mouth with my little finger to let drops of milk fall down for you to swallow without any impediment. Hours and hours, I bent over with you so that you could feed on the greatest love that exists, your mother's. Dad could not touch you, nor could your brothers come close. I disinfected myself and loved you in every delicate word I said to you, you with those big eyes -because you only had eyes- that looked at me for a second and closed themselves immediately, without strength, invaded by the sedative and painful anticipation of your birth. But May came and with it came the Pentecost festivities in Bellavista de la Jara, and we went to the village. Then, and almost miraculously, you had put on weight; you were the most beautiful girl in the world and I made you some beautiful robes that grandma embroidered; and with your flirtatious little face you looked at any passerby, family or stranger, seeking a caress. I knew I was capable of filling you with my love, my daughter."

I embraced her with all the love I was capable of.

"Mom, thank you, thank you, thank you, a thousand times and as many times as it takes. Thank you for being so brave, for being so immense, for being such a mother."

Sara would not be Sara without that exemplified love elevated to the maximum power; she could not be a mother without having suckled motherhood even before the stars had decided that it should be so. It is through the blinding clarity which comes with the passing of time that I am able to understand why there was, in the deepest part of my soul, the serious and peremptory right, as well as the need, to be a mother.

"So many times, I was told that I would not have children because of my ovaries. So many, many times I cried imagining that such a joy would never be mine. But now when I look at you, I still thank God for blessing me with you, my children. And if you ever extend the lineage, remember that, in your genetic history, in your village history, there is a saga of mothers, not selfless, but immensely happy to be so."

That night, which should have had no end, that should have been eternal, had its dawn. It was loaded with a living testament of confidences, gratitudes, surprises and solved enigmas; stories that made me understand who Ana was; who, beyond being a mother, was seen in my eyes for the first time as a woman who loved, desired, suffered and decided at every moment to live life quintessentially. I knew of her weaknesses, even her failures or character flaws, of her dislike of lies, of her need to extol her self-esteem, and perhaps most importantly, her never allowing anyone or anything to make her stop being herself.

That Holy Wednesday morning, Ana prayed with Manuel and her children. The hospital chaplain arrived and gave her the sacrament of the anointing of the sick, which she received with an astonishing serenity. It is true, she was afraid, but she did not show it. She looked at Manuel and smiled with that face of hers that made him wink at her, even though she was already tired at her now eighty years of age. The priest left and we all remained in a dense and opaque silence. Soon the orderlies would take her away to begin the most difficult battle.

"Dad, you haven't eaten for five long hours, it's time you did as you need food. Besides, we were told it would be long and laborious.

"Sara, I can't eat."

"Shall we both have a juice, then? Come with me, we'll go for a walk and stretch our legs and relieve the aching of the mind that is tearing us apart."

The walk through the different rooms through which Sara and Manuel passed was increasingly tiring for Manuel; his back curved by osteoarthritis, whose wily needle every so often pierced causing him to cry out in pain; and his slow pace due to the lack of news. His tear-streaked eyes would, from time to time, look into Sara's in search of answers, to which Sara responded with the most compassionate look she was capable of. And so, two more hours passed, when suddenly the double doors of the operating room opened, and two surgeons came out with the call of "Ana's relatives". Suddenly, the emptiness in the pit of the stomach that causes this and other internal organs to rise to your throat left his lungs without any breath; his heart stopped beating for a few seconds; his brain understood that he had to be lucid in order to understand clearly everything that would be said to him, as well as what he needed to ask. But Manuel was unable to utter a sound.

"That's us! Excuse us, we're on our way, but my father has to go slowly."

"Don't worry, but, Manuel, is that you? I can't believe we operated on Ana without knowing it was her, for God's sake!"

"That's normal," said Sara, "you don't waste time looking them in the eyes to identify if it is person A or B. You have to operate mechanically, leaving aside the sentimental ties that bind us to the soul of another person. The important thing is that you do what is in your hands to save us from the poison of cancer, no matter who it is. Please, we need to know."

"The situation has been very complicated. The seriousness of your mother's cancer was greater than the medical tests had led us to suspect. We have had to remove more of the lungs than is desirable. In addition, she suffered a heart attack. But she is stable now, and she will be taken to the ICU, where she will receive the best care. From now on, and especially over the next 24 hours, it will be the anesthesiologist and the critical care specialists who will keep you informed."

"Is there hope?" inquired Manuel in an almost inaudible voice, out of tune with the clearing of his dry throat. He was dwarfed by grief and the fear that he was going to hear what his intuition was telling him.

"Manuel, let's see how it goes over the next few hours. Don't worry, everything will be fine."

"Can we see her? Please."

"Go ahead. But only two people, Manuel and you, Sara. She is still sedated."

Manuel, stunned and shocked, did not recognize her.

"Ana, Ana, my dearest and most beloved Ana...."

Even I, her soul child, was not able to look at her straight. The mixture of "why did they have to leave you like this" with "please, fight with all your strength and win the battle", ran over with "listen to me, Mom, I love you with all my heart, don't leave me alone, not now".

The nurses quickly pulled us away because the grief and tears were not helpful to the patient whose semi-consciousness could be altered. So, in no time at all an orderly rushed to her bedside and carried her away without another word.

The ICU waiting room was a long corridor where relatives of all kinds of patients exchanged words of support, as well as fictitious hopes. Because good news was short-lived, we told each other what had caused our loved ones to be there; but who cares if it was an operation, accident, heart attack, stroke... we all gradually lost strength because someone we desperately loved was trapped in those cubicles separated by dirty white and metal screens.

On the first visit, two by two, in silence, we were given the instructions about hygiene, sounds and treatment that we had to follow to the letter. That's how everybody came in. Manuel remained inside all the time, until I went in. "That monster with half-open eyes is you, Mom," I thought, swallowing my breath and questioning if things like that made sense in life. A pang in my chest brought me back from my reverie, putting the nightmare aside to approach her headboard. I kissed her forehead and a little piece of forearm that was free of needles and wires. I hoped with fervent belief that she was able to hear me, because moving her pretty lips was quite impossible with the huge tube that ran down her throat and trachea from apex to apex.

It cannot be true that she is conscious, they cannot have a person with the anxiety and knowledge of noticing a tube that does not allow you to move your neck, talk, salivate, eat, kiss. What an inhuman way of healing is this? Galloping injustices were crowding in each successive or superimposed thought. I was not able to digest what that bunch of specialists was doing to her. Feelings were multiplying in my tummy and shooting out of my ears like the valve of a pressure cooker. I had to blame someone, obligatorily and stubbornly I had to blame someone for what I considered harmful actions without any kind of justification. When I got home, waiting for the phone to ring for an emergency or to make a prelude to something, I was aware that time can be measured in its most extensive length and sense of its duration, because the hours were eternal, the seconds had infinite tenths of a second; but the ticking of the clock and its hands made the dawn arrive, to wait again until noon, when the first visits to the hospital took place.

So, Friday, March 25, Good Friday, arrived. After seeing Our Lord Jesus of Nazareth and having a birthday coffee, I went down to the famous ICU unit. Already seasoned and brilliant first-class students, we did as we were told and complied with all the instructions to go in to visit Mom. But this time, my desire to be recognized by her was even more penetrating. I, her daughter, had a birthday, and she, my mother, could not remain as a sleeping beauty waiting to wake up from her induced reverie. She had to do the impossible: to recover, to learn to breathe without the help of any device to take air into her lungs; and most importantly, she had to do it because I needed her. Love or selfishness? What difference does it make, when both coexist in the body, meet, dance, push or swim under the same current. It is absurd to question what we really feel, when what is clear to us is that she should wake up and breathe for herself.

"Mom, it's me, Sara, open your eyes, please."

Ana opened her eyes with a sleepy look.

"Mom, do you know what day it is today? I'm sure you haven't noticed, but it's Good Friday and my birthday. I'm holding your little hand, if you're listening to me, squeeze my fingers a little bit. Come on, be brave and do it!"

And Ana gently squeezed my hand and tried to open her eyes wider.

"I know you can hear me and you know what I'm telling you. You are going to recover. They must keep the tube in so you can breathe better, but it's only for a few days. Don't despair, you are in the best hands, and I know how strong you are, so let yourself go, everything will be fine, I promise."

During the ten short minutes I was with her I took the opportunity to kiss her wherever that swarm of wires and tracks allowed me to. I couldn't cry, but I could feel how the collar of my shirt was getting wetter and wetter. The smell of her skin, her smell, the one I'd adored since I was a little girl, was mixed with that indescribable but easily recognizable smell of alcohol, iodine, medication, hospital. But it was still her, my beloved and adored mother.

A nurse came in, it was time to leave the cubicle, my Ana's healing den. As we were leaving, the specialist who was on duty made us enter that cold room to tell us that they were going to try to remove the hated and life-saving tube. The emotion for a few seconds intoxicated our lives, there was then hope, although the but that came later was a cold-water pitcher. They were going to try, which did not mean that it would be successful. We had to return home where the hours languished waiting, waiting, waiting.

It was six o'clock in the evening when we again followed our particular Way of the Cross to her cubicle. When we entered, instead of the huge tube that broke her beautiful neck, she had a small tube that reminded us of a soft straw like the ones they sell with colored sugar in candy stores. Her serene countenance suggested that the agony of the previous state had ceased, but in truth she was sedated. We did not know that a quarter of an hour before she had had a heart attack. And that is where it really hurts the soul, when you see treatment, they have to give her to anchor her in this life, which from what we were seeing, belonged less and less to her.

And then came the moment, the one you are never ready to face.

"Sara, run to the cubicle, Mom is babbling something we can't understand."

"Mom, it's Sara, tell me what's wrong."

Ana looked towards the window and lifted her chin. I asked her if she wanted me to open it, to which she nodded with a gesture of desperation. I went to the window, pretending to do as she asked, because the window was wide open. She was choking.

Without saying a word, I went to the nurse standing at the door watching the scene and begged him,

"For God's sake, my mother is drowning, help me."

"Your mother is dying, there is no hope. She has been semiconscious for three days, suffering real tragedies for us to save a life that without that machine would not have existed for days, you must make a decision and give her a dignified death."

No, it was not possible. It was not because of that tube that my mother was alive, but because of her will. My mother was conscious. It was not possible that she knew what was really waiting for her. "Noooooo!" I screamed silently, drowned in a cry that was unable to leave my body, petrified and scared to death for not knowing how to tell her Manuel. What do I have to do? Is it Christian to have the machines taken away from her? She is my mother, don't you understand?

Manuel looked at me with those eyes of defeat that see no light anywhere. Very slowly I took him to the old bench at the door of the hospital, my brothers following in silent procession. They were waiting for me to get to the point where I could explain to them.

"Dad, Mom is not really breathing on her own. Since the day of the operation the induced breathing is the only thing that has kept her heart afloat, but if that machine shuts down, she will fly out of our nest."

"Sara..." The crying and pain in his soul did not allow him to continue.

"Dad, we must be strong now, we have to say goodbye to her with a free soul. We cannot take shelter in her soul, she must go to the Heavenly Father, we have to let her go to her repose. All they are doing with her is prolonging a conscious and inhuman agony. Dad, the window was wide open and..." I collapsed, I could not go on, there were no more explanations to give, only to wait.

The four of us hugged, squeezed each other and in that instant, we were called. The scene blurs my eyes, but it is clear in my mind. Ana, with her hair combed and her lips shiny from the Vaseline that had been put there, sitting up in bed, her eyes serene and full of life. We approached her bed, Manuel next to her head, me at the height of her hand and my brothers caressing her legs. We had only two minutes to say goodbye, Ana, my mother of my soul. Only two minutes to thank you for giving us that immense and intense love that only you knew how to give. Two minutes to ask you for forgiveness for everything we should have done for you; two minutes to beg you not to abandon us, wherever you went; two minutes for the rest of our lives just to be able to remember you.

Her gaze was extinguished and she was gone forever.

To the glory of God for my dear wife Ana.

My dear and beloved Ana,

As always, I express my love for you, because thanks to Him we have enjoyed a lifetime, until He considered that it was the exact time to take you to His side. But you must know that my love for you increases day by day, without limit, without any obstacle. And that love fills me with an intense faith that makes me desire even more to love God through you.

All my actions are done thinking of you. I reflect and think of your perfect know-how and how I act under your criteria with our children and grandchildren. You know the difference in our characters, but I try to look at them as you did, as you taught me every day, putting yourself in their shoes and filing corners with that parental love that you have forced me to adopt since your departure.

I ask you to intercede for each of our three children, and for our Sara, who has gone as far as to write a book of the story of her shared history, in which you are one of the most essential parts. In writing the book about our family, in novel form, she has made me remember each of the most important moments I shared with you. It has helped her find the answers about her innermost being and made me realize that I didn't love you enough, because this love, right from that first letter is the most beautiful thing I could ever experience.

Since that March 31st, I always make the same request of you: "guide me in every act and decision, and continue to do it until I reach you and my soul merges again with yours, as our love did so many times".

As a farewell, receive my great love through the love I profess to God, for He in His omnipotence will send it to you.

My life by your side goes on in that virtual way, in which thinking about you and adoring you is my way of breathing and nourishing myself.

I love you, my dearest and most beloved Ana, from that first kiss to this last letter.

Always yours.

Manuel

I can't go on. It's so hard, even after almost three years. I can't, Mom. I can't remember your appearance; I have to do it in the absence of space, without your voice, without your smell, without your soft skin, without the touch of your hair, without your little smile." I can't, Mom. I miss you so much. Each word is a torn sentence because I love you; because I miss you so much; because I live and sometimes, I die when I can't tell you what happens to me, what I feel. My God, I love you, Mom!

Sara, January 2019.

Chapter XXI
In search of my truth

I know why I now question my own essence from my reality, because my person is the result of more lives that, before mine, have already changed realities.

Perhaps it was not coherent to see the cause of my rootlessness in me, without really knowing where I belong, but now I know. I belong to those stories told in previous chapters; they are not narrated just for the sake of it. It is time to reveal why Angela and Ana make me feel the way I am, looking for the essence of my own soul. That is why it is time to talk about me, Sara Almena de la Vega, about the Almena and de la Vega saga; families whose love was the path they chose in all their decisions, besides the honor and all the values rooted in those times.

Reaching this point, where I perform the most intense striptease I could imagine in all my vital, emotional, mental bodies; clinging to the bar of ancestral memories; wiggling to the sound of the melody of love; stripping off every garment without apparent modesty; seducing, winking, watching, intriguing or insolently discovering those intimate parts that we all share but which so few of us dare to show, has not been easy.

A few months ago, looking for documents in my parents' house, I discovered one of those faded folders with the elastic bands removed, which was hidden, perhaps abandoned, at the bottom of a drawer. It caught my attention and I started to flick through it with the creeping sensation of doing something forbidden. When I least expected it and in the middle of committing my unconscious crime, my father came into the study and scolded me because I had opened it and was shuffling through its papers. After a few seconds, during which his eyes were fixed on me as when I was a child and he caught me red-handed, we both sat very close at the desk in his study. He looked me in the eyes and hugged me and I felt his smell, that unmistakable scent of my dad, that feeling of being loved without equal, that you feel when your father cuddles you to his chest. I didn't understand his emotion until I saw the contents of the old folder. Though the exterior was stale and obsolete, its interior was fascinating. It was like opening a box of chocolates. When I began to read, the feeling was very complex: the need to know oh so many things, among them the lives of others; events that I would never have questioned if I had not opened that old folder. That was my father's gift to me, which he had not found the time to give me: "my treasure". He knew that, for me, that folder contained the necessary pointers for me to find myself and decide my destiny. Would I really find out why I am like this? In it were those hallowed letters and documents, which from the beginning gave me goosebumps, that have made me find out the depths of Angela and Ana's past lives in the intense search for the reason why I feel the way I do about life. And there was also my birth certificate and the letters I wrote Manuel and Ana when I was a child.

I was born in Madrid on March 25, 1972, a Saturday, at ten o'clock in the morning, after just seven months and with a laziness that did not allow me to reveal the warrior in me. But there was another warrior, far stronger than me, my mother Ana who, with her love and tireless vigilance, made me thrive, drop by drop of milk, without caring about the time or anything else but full love.

After two years, Manuel was moved to Jaen, and that is where I have my memories. My childhood was spent in Bellavista de la Jara on weekends and during holidays and in Jaen during the week. I just remember those Palm Sundays in the village, when we wore the mini outfits that our grandmothers and mothers made for us, not always to the right size and with material that sometimes itched, ha, ha, ha, ha. Those crocheted panties which, when the elastic was gone, you didn't know if they were someone else's or your own; and those socks so tight at the calf, whose elastic was embedded leaving a great tattoo that stung like hell and lasted till the next day.

I remember, as if it were yesterday, those noon-times with the sun overhead, that made the fieriness of that blood-red land shine even more, and that attracted you with the greatest temptation to let yourself slip, like a slide, down the slopes of its mountains, although the results on the dress and underwear were really disastrous and conclusive evidence of the crime.

My childhood was happy. I was loved and protected by my parents, in those magical and dark houses of my grandparents, where the forbidden made my eagerness to be a detective overcome my childhood terrors. When I was eight years old, I went up to the chambers of grandfather Samuel's house for the first time. It was the eve of Epiphany, and I was sick with the mumps. The adults had gone shopping while I stayed in the room that overlooked a small landing, from which opened the door to a paradise of the unknown. I put on my slippers, put on a long cardigan and set out to go upstairs. As it is normal being alone and walking towards the unknown my heart was beating at two thousand beats a minute. I arrived and shivered from the cold, but far from shrinking, the adventurer in me made me walk towards a trunk that was next to a window, which I remember as being low, almost from the ground and with a grille. Slowly I put my little hands on the latch of the trunk and moved it. There was dust. I opened it and there they were; I fell in love as soon as I saw them, which nowadays has no merit, since shoes are my passion, but those black shoes with patterns engraved on their leather like the most perfect leather goods made me think that I was one of those ladies from the thirties, maybe an infiltrator in the most dangerous and forbidden place in the world. I put them on, but the floor sounded hollow and I was afraid of being discovered. I looked at them on my little feet and contemplated, it was the first time I put on a pair of high heels. Suddenly, I heard,

"Sara, where are you?"

They had already caught me. I had to wake up from my reverie. My mother was calling me anxiously and I was going to be caught red-handed. I had to put those shoes in the right place, close the trunk and go downstairs fully alert, go through the rooms on the left to the bathroom and sit on the icy toilet. I got downstairs very quietly, closed the door, went through the rooms on the left, my plan was working as expected, I opened the door of the last bedroom, what a joy in me, I was a fantastic strategist! And when I slowly turned the doorknob, there she was, my mother, up in arms and questioning me with her angry mother eyes, the thousand questions of all mothers: "Where were you? Why didn't you answer? What were you doing?". And, of course, the direct threat: "If you lie to me, you'll kill me and you'll lose your gift from the Kings! But no, I was not left without my gift, they gave me the "Miss Pepi's briefcase" with all the pots and makeup brushes I wanted. How capricious life is! Almost forty years remembering those shoes and it is now, remembering them with my father, when I learn that those heels belonged to my grandmother Angela. Maybe it is nonsense, or maybe not, because those shoes have accompanied me in my dreams and in my thoughts since that moment.

The nights of Epiphany, sweet smells and hopes. Now I understand why my parents always made it magical, the impeccable routine of cleaning the shoes, putting them in the long hallway next to the bedrooms. The smell of the ring shaped cake that my mother kneaded with its bean and its surprise coin inside, the tradition of not being able to eat it until the parade had passed in front of the house, salivating, knowing the piece with chocolate that was waiting for me next to the nativity scene that my mother lovingly placed on the bridge of the Immaculate Conception.

Twelfth Night, generations of children and adults with that indescribable feeling of infantile fear, expectation and uncertainty for what could happen that night. The surprise of waking up earlier than expected to find the shoes with the longed-for toys, the candies and, on occasion, the sweet coal for not having been as good as I should have been.

But not everything in my childhood was happiness. I soon discovered how pain made my mother stop being her. Ana never felt she had a physical defect, she never let her foot be a problem, until I was eight years old – 1980 was a special year in my childhood. My mother limped and it hurt more and more, the cramps and pins and needles left her barely breathing, she was given special insoles and always wore orthopedic shoes.

One day my parents left for Cordoba. They were nervous before their departure. My mother gave me orders without rhyme or reason, my father rushed her and told her that they would be late. I had just come from school and she was putting on her makeup and combing her hair in the bathroom. I sat on the toilet seat and watched her quietly so as not to get in the way. I was always fascinated to see the ritual of her makeup, light and delicate, but which made her more and more beautiful, and that gesture she made with the lipstick when she finished applying that mixture of her two favorite lipsticks.

She looked at me through the mirror and gave me one of her little smiles, the kind that tells you, "it's all right, nothing's wrong!". I got up and hugged her from behind, she turned and kissed me on my hair, those kisses that bring the smell of mom and her perfect warmth, and that calm that only a mother, who protects her chick like a broody hen, gives.

The trip to Cordoba would change our lives. A wonderful polio surgeon, who worked at the Red Cross hospital, was going to see them, run the appropriate tests and determine if Mom's condition had a chance of being cured; if not, perhaps she would have to admit that she would end up in a wheelchair.

"Ana, how are you feeling? I hope and pray you are not nervous. I have some news to tell you."

"Don Miguel, without beating around the bush, I have already been told on countless occasions that there is no solution, because pregnancies and the passing of the years have made my foot more and more overturned. I am ready."

"Ana, after the tests and exploration I did, I will operate. I cannot ensure the outcome. In fact, you may end up in a wheelchair earlier if it goes wrong, but I see that you have good muscles and circulation. I am going to completely undo your foot, insert a pin from the heel and I am going to do a puzzle with your bones and muscles."

"Don Miguel, wait. Are you sure there is a chance of improvement?"

"Yes, Ana, but it will be very long and painful."

"Don Miguel, when will you operate on me?"

In a week the miracle was done; said and done. In the month of October Don Miguel operated on her; about eight hours in the operating room, three months bedridden, a year without help; and, thank you, my God, for never bringing a wheelchair into the house!"

But what I am telling in a few lines changed my perception of her. The week before she was doing her makeup in the blue bathroom and now she could not move. The pains were so strong that sometimes she could not even approach me. She stopped going to school to pick me up; she stopped making her loving meals; she stopped being her. Now, with the passing of the years, I am aware that was when I began to feel guilty for not being perfect for her. I wanted to be older, to help her, to be her support, but I was still a child who, when I wanted to be that chattering girl and tell her about my adventures and misadventures at school, was in the way. Aunt Irene would tell me to get out and not bother her. Then I would go into my room, close the door and ask God to please cure her and give me back my mother.

When her cast was removed and she started to walk, we went up to the Parador. I love those pictures, because that day I started to feel that I had recovered my mommy, and that maybe my wish to see her walking in high heels would come true.

Remembering my childhood also takes me back to her first love. An evocation comes to my mind, when sitting in the kitchen: on an afternoon of confessions, when she told me I was grown up enough to share the secret of when she discovered her first love. Her eyes lit up as she reminisced on that first glance, no doubt also remembering the strictness of her upbringing and her mother's views on boys.

It was impossible for you, Ana, to feel good about yourself, when the mere act of looking was little more than blasphemy. And it is now, at forty-five years old, when I understand you in the deepest part of my being more than ever, I know that my daughter cannot go through what Fatima, you, and even I went through. It is time to empower the feelings of the need to be oneself and, from the greatness of understanding that love well understood -starting with oneself- is much more than life itself, because it is the path that will cement passions and future loves.

And it is because of all of the above that I no longer question why when we like someone, we deny it. My awakening to love was also like that. I also felt those sensations for the first time when I was twelve years old. It was in summer -almost all those first sensations occur in spring or summer- in Bellavista de la Jara. I went to play in the garden of the Ermita and there was a boy, Mario, a cousin of one of my friends. We played "cops and robbers" and when he found me and looked me in the eyes, time and space stopped; I floated like a fool and I began to notice how a suffocating heat ran through my chest and back. I realized that I wasn't looking at him the same way as before and that it no longer went unnoticed. I reacted all weird to an unfamiliar sensation. I was quickly transported to that place of arrogance and pride that makes you act defensively, with disdain, as if we don't care about the strangeness we are perceiving, while inside we are melting, restless, expectant and wishing they were still looking at us or talking to us. However, as the song says, we get "proud and haughty", yet batting our eyelashes in perfect harmony with the beating of our heart.

And it is right now, when my thirteen-year-old little girl is discovering that her heart races when suddenly a boy, perhaps not the most handsome, looks at her or smiles at her, three generations of women and the same feeling, the first love or, better said, the awakening to love.

And again, love shows me that I don't know everything about it, because it makes me very upset to think that my daughter, my doll, is feeling what they call "first love", and you say to yourself: "it can't be! You still play with your things in your room. How can it be that now you are floating in love like a fool?". But it is so and I must accept it, and I want her to be happy because she is growing up and doing it in a radiant and healthy way.

And now, at my age, with all that entails, I am left with love and all its nuances from the beginning to the end.

Many times during my adolescence, I heard the phrase "butterflies' wings burn when you touch them". But when my father or my mother said it to me, it made me angry and I became defensive like a little panther, because deep down, like everyone else, I wanted and, somehow, I needed, to be liked. Not only by the boy I liked, but also my elders, my friends, my teachers. There came a time when I lived more for what others wanted from me than for myself. It was in this state of dependence that I began to write "I am like this", without any rhyme or reason. I did not know why, when I let myself be carried away by this phrase, I felt much better, but it is true that this statement made me see myself with different eyes and not as dependent. Anyway, today I am discovering why I am like this and, unlike then, I do not seek to please because I feel the need or require it; now I do things with the deep feeling of doing them, because I believe in myself, and the truth, whatever the result, that makes me feel "awesome". But it has been difficult to correct that feeling empowered by my subconscious, because every time I thought of something that would make me happy, it was accompanied by feelings of guilt over the selfishness involved; wanting something for myself, or valuing myself, meant self-centeredness and vanity. How little we have been left to value ourselves, yet how necessary it is! But I thank my parents and grandparents once and a thousand times, because their values also had, as everything in life, many positive things, and the mixture of what is rooted with what is accepted and positivized, make my life very different today. The road is not easy, but the reward will be incredible.

To suddenly imagine how our parents could be in love is something that surpasses us; just as to conjecture how their intimate relationships would be, is something so unimaginable that we have all said at one time or another, "the stork brought me". Our parents are so because they are, period. Stopping to think about such things is not viable as it is to take away the focus on their being parents. But the truth is that our parents at some point in their lives were teenagers, young people full of life and hopes, passionate and with the madness of the moment as the limits allowed.

So, how will my daughter see me? Oh, rough terrain! I remember the moment when I stopped seeing my parents as the gods of Olympus, to become, simply, my parents, those two beings who made me feel ridiculous at family gatherings, either because they made me feel more childish than I was, or because they told some anecdote in which I came out not very favorably. Being a teenager is sometimes unbearable, because you feel capable, mature, a woman, and then your parents remind you, seemingly every moment, that you are not; because you still do not pick up or tidy your room as you should, because you cannot go out; because the phone does not pay for itself and it is for emergencies, and "what is so important that you have tell your friend when you just left her five minutes ago?" But at the same time, in adolescence you feel the first tingling in the belly, the first feeling of attraction, the first real fights with friends and the first conscious need to be liked by others. A thousand times thank you to my parents, for being bad parents in adolescence, because it meant nothing other than loving me intensely.

In my life there have also been lies: my own and others'. But we all lie, and I ask myself: Have I ever gauged the consequences of a lie? Do you gauge them?

I read an article in the *National Geographic*, May 24, 2017, about lying. It stated the causes as: hiding a fact, financial gain, personal gain, avoidance, false acceptance. Goleman in his book *The Blind Spot*, on the psychology of self-deception, says,

"...the mind can protect itself from anxiety by lowering awareness. A blind spot is created, an area where we are prone to block our attention and self-deception."

I remember the first moment in which I felt I was Ana's accomplice. It was when I was about twenty-three years old. We were in front of the Blessed Virgin, and when my mother turned around there was Juan Antonio, her childhood boyfriend, standing like a statue and staring at her, adoring her without saying anything. He looked at me and greeted my mother with "Your daughter is as beautiful as you, but she looks more like her father. She could have been our daughter."

"Swallow me, earth," I thought at that moment. "Who is this fool? How dare he? I'm going to give him what for." But I didn't have time. My mother, with one of those tender and sweet smiles that illuminated whatever room she was in, answered for me,

"I am very happy to see you. I hope you and your family are doing well and that you have been able to forgive me."

The tangle between the three of us caused the conversation to end in a sweet silence. Juan Antonio kissed my mother on the cheek followed by a sigh, inhaling her perfume and filling himself with the memory that those sensations produced in him. My mother, however, felt the joy of seeing that he was well and that she had been forgiven; finally, I, your narrator, was unsettled and immersed in a single thought: my mother had been loved by someone else; my mother's decision had done harm; my mother was not only my mother, she was a woman.

I love that memory, that instant in which she was desired, she was admired, even in the way she was the impossible love of Juan

Antonio; but also, her sustained shame, her desire to minimize what happened, her determination to forget it, made me see her as a woman who defends her decision, even if she had caused harm with it.

The wink she gave me when Juan Antonio told me that I could have been his daughter shook my mind; to think that my mother could be his wife and I his daughter, having had a completely different life, a different father, different siblings, a house in another place. A hurricane of thoughts was tangled like a skein. But the strangest thing of all was that I did not feel bad, I did not blame my mother, I was simply carried away by the prospect of being the consequence of my mother having made different decision.

Our decisions have a direct consequence on our future; taking one path or another, making life reciprocate with constant sermons until you find the right path; being aware that lies blur the future and that those who follow the path of the heart, never make mistakes. As Aute used to say: "The truth is never so sad that it has no remedy".

The lie came later, when my mother, looking at the floor, asked me to keep that conversation to myself. But in the end, as expected, she herself confessed the encounter to Manuel, and his response was as expected,

"But who does he think he is? Look, Ana, I don't like him talking to you."

When I think of those years of childhood and youth, not so distant in my mind as in years, my mind recollects my first heartbreak. It happened to Angela and Ana, but they ended up marrying their loves; in my case it was quite different. I fell in love with his eyes, his stature, his smiles, his jokes, and in my eyes, he was Prince Charming! But the ecstasy was short-lived. His eagerness to conquer other ports made the wind erase him from my sight in less time than a rooster crows. And that was how I tried to forget that love for the first time with another love, something that rarely works, at least for me. I kept longing for the person I really loved; I hated his attitude and even his memories; I changed my hairstyle and even bought new clothes, rather dead than plain; I looked for a new perfume -at that time Don Algodón- and I repeated to myself a thousand times "you are already forgotten". But I was dying inside and, if he had been within my reach, I would have given him one of those epoch-making speeches, asserting myself and showing him everything he had lost, like the brave heifer that was always tearing herself away inside me. Though scorned and scorned, I kept quiet and kept looking for unconscious similarities in the green mulberry to silence the shrieks of the broken heart.

It was over. I didn't have to keep quiet anymore. I was the owner of my "life". I could decide. The eternal Penelope shook her hair and put on her jeans. The first change I felt was my need to say what I openly thought. I didn't have to keep my feelings quiet. I could say what I wanted to or not. It was at the end of the nineties, I and the women around me began to declare our thoughts and feelings freely, we expressed our desires without open judgment -if there was any, we didn't care- and that was wonderful, because we, women in general, became aware, and more and more so. But as everything has its upside and downside, along the way we have also been losing that romanticism in which the man sought the charms to delight the heart of his beloved, because we decided to be the ones who took the step without waiting a minute more.

Yes, now I miss that courtship. After the liberation of expressing whatever I want, I miss that not knowing what will happen after the first call, the first date, first WhatsApp, will he will call me; will he ask me to give him my voice; will he grant me an afternoon walk in which I can jump puddles like a girl and get soaked with a sprinkler in the middle of the lawn of the park; will he think I'm crazy for singing *Dying of love* loudly in the car; or will he decide to surprise me with a meal, served with a white rose, garnished with words that come together to express so much as I wait to hear from his lips something like "you are my all"?

This reminds me of one of my favorite movies, *Love Has Two Faces*, from 1996. Yes, I like that part where Rose tells her students: "When we fall in love, we hear Puccini in our hearts, we don't know how it will happen or how long it will last, but it feels great!"

It's true, I am a romantic. First lesson learned from my generational history, I have to be, having had a grandfather who lived his feelings with such intensity. The best thing about this, my first step, is that I am neither ashamed nor will I cover it up for the rest of my days.

I'm romantic and I want everything, everything, everything.

Chapter XXIII
Love me always

One extremely hot, early September afternoon, David knocked on my apartment door. I was barefoot, in my T-shirt and underwear, disheveled and sticky from the heat of my nap. I didn't look through the peephole, I opened the door and turned around inviting my neighbor to come in while I went straight to the couch, when, as if on cue, I heard his voice. Embarrassed by the situation and the way I looked, my rather skimpy inappropriate attire, not waiting for him to come in and not knowing what to say, I retreated into a mess of embarrassment. The whirlwind of questions merged into a single thought, "it's him", which circumscribed the situation between comical, absurd, out of place and, in every way, unexpected.

I was not able to turn around, I wanted to run to my room to clean myself up a bit, but I was paralyzed. He approached me from behind and as soon as I felt the touch of his hands on my shoulders I ran to my room, slamming the door. I sat on the bed and began to cry like an inconsolable fool. But why was I doing it? It was ridiculous; both me and the situation.

I got up about ten times, taking a thousand outfits out of the closet, until, in an instant, I looked at myself in the mirror, scared to death, but what did it matter, if I was like that? I was also a sobbing T-shirt and panties, barefoot and disheveled girl. What rancor and desire for revenge! A thousand conflicting feelings in the roller coaster that was my being. Why would he have come? I was content with my day-to-day life. I had decided to pass on winning the Olympic medal of his love. It hurt, yes; but the time had passed without pain or glory. Now he was coming to my house. For what? I wasn't going to get dressed; but if I didn't, I was going to look a mess; so, maybe, though I didn't know why, it would be better if I dressed up a little. What the hell! I wasn't going to do it! I would come out haughty; I was a tough woman; no crying, no bullshit. He always came back with his "it wasn't me" face and then did whatever he wanted. His commitments! I laughed at so many stories to keep me hooked, tales and fables with only one moral: "I have you at my beck and call". But what was he telling me, if I was crazy about him? Absurd, a thousand times absurd! Neither with you nor without you, the dog in the manger, that's what I was. It was over! I had to go out and speak to him very clearly. He wasn't going to play with me for another minute.

"What have you come for?" I said, opening the door with the same look and the snot hanging from my nose, but with my guts in my mouth.

"I need to talk to you. You are a sight for sore eyes!" he said jocularly.

"Well, don't look at me if it bothers you so much. Just tell me what you have to tell me and go away. I'm busy."

"Sara, I have no more commitments, I want to be with you."

"Now you come to me with that?" I said pointing at him with my index finger. "All summer making me crazy, without doing anything to take it any further. Do you want me to remind you what happened after my accident? You helped me, of course you helped me, but you also left my heart half-battered again. You're gaslighting," I finished raising my tone and growing in every one of those words. "You give one spoon of sugar and another of sand. You are not consistent. You drive my heart crazy and you tear me apart. I'm fed up with meaningless and endless games. Please, get the hell out of my house, and this time for good."

"Sara, stop it, don't keep on scolding me. I told you I would take the step or I would leave forever. I have taken the step."

"And I'm supposed to believe you?" I asked with a wry chuckle, "of course, I must do it because you are you, the lord who dominates everything, who can do everything. Have you ever wondered if you are really capable of making me happy? If you are up to giving me everything I want? If you are really smart enough to look beyond your nose? If..." I said pointing to the door.

"It's over, Sara," he interrupted.

David pounced on me, grabbed me by my shirt and kissed me. He kissed me like no one had ever kissed me before. I was aware that he had the exhilarating virtue of turning me on, with just one kiss splashed with pent-up desire, in the narrow span of three seconds. His lips pressed against mine, eagerly possessing them. His stubbornly eager tongue sought mine, in an unconscious effort to take it into his mouth, to make it his. His hands slid energetically over my back, my buttocks, my thighs, almost causing me pain with his trembling fingers, but that sweet hurt made me want more and more. His body glued to mine denoted how his desire was growing; it was no longer his, he belonged to me and I no longer belonged to him. I only obeyed the clamor of a passion contained for months and months, from April to September, a gale, in short, an emotional and sexual tsunami.

Every second had a caress of its own, an uncontained moan that came out in every exhalation we allowed ourselves. I wanted to stop, my mind would not allow me to continue, but my body responded, I am yours and you are mine. I wanted him to possess me, colonize me and build the pleasure that the moment itself gave us.

Without any lull, we were devoted to the discovery of our bodies. His hands had no other place to lodge than in my sensual breasts longing for his kisses, giving them to him as spoils of war to his tireless movements, awakening with every touch to the seduction and madness that he provoked in me. My hands searching for the most evident sign of his desire, the grip of my caresses that provoked in him a huge ardor and vigor, breathless, but delivered to our silent love. We were approaching the place where there is no time or space, where the magic of having achieved the desired gave way to the delivery, and the delivery to possession, saying goodbye to the rest of the clothes and skin that wrapped our lives, we arrived at the bed.

David changed the incoherent rhythm of his passion, slowing down his craving for sex, looking carefully into my eyes, his mouth red from the struggle. Seconds that discolored me for an eternal instant. I closed and opened my eyes in the most expressive interrogation and he began again to kiss me with a soft whisper, "I'm going to make you mine. I love you Sara".

His hands navigated through the silk of my face, they went down to my neck stopping at the curves of my breasts, on tiptoe and flirting with my skin they brushed my belly to go fast towards my legs; his caresses took me to that dream from which you do not want to wake up; he made his way through the walls of my slopes and possessed me, and with all the love in the world, he made me his, again and again, until the lights of dawn gave us a new life.

We awakened in the dawn of an unexpected beginning, but no less desired. The days and months went by with furtive encounters, exciting messages and a game of passion and tenderness that entangled us in the blanket that was woven with our love.

A year passed, with all its seasons, but the temperature was the same: it was always warm between us. The conversations without let up, the destinations full of laughter and caresses, the desire that we both gave each other.

"I love this place, what strength and magnetism it has."

"Can you hear them?"

"How could anyone not hear them! What a bellowing they make, they're going to leave them dry," he said with a chuckle.

"I'm going to leave you if you keep looking at me with those naughty eyes."

"Come on, you exaggerator, it's not like you're Andalusian!"

"What's the name of this place?"

"Quintos de Mora."

"I even like the name, it's brutal what the deer provoke in me with their rutting. Look, they're sticking together, they're going to intertwine their antlers if they keep it up. They pull away to come back in a visceral race until their heads meet. But if they hook their antlers they're going to die."

"Sometimes it happens. It is not usual, but when they toss against each other they come to be caught in such a way that they cannot be separated and death is agonizing."

"It's crazy, the youngest one is pushing away, the strongest against the veteran, all with only one goal, to get the damsels. You know?"

"What?"

"My dream, David, is to go to Africa, I would like to go on a photographic safari, to experience its intensity, its fragrance, its magnetism, the colors, the colorfulness and arrogance of its animals."

"What? You want to go to Africa? Sara, marry me and let's go together. A declaration impregnated with dreams and adventures, a desire linked to the clichés of society, marriage and a spectacular honeymoon, after the purchase of a semi-detached house and a nice car."

And thus it was done: a wonderful townhouse for us, full-fledged wedding and honeymoon with gifts included, return with more crew, my own baby girl was already in charge without my even knowing it.

I had the complete package, and anything other than happiness and contentment would have been ingratitude. It was the happy fairytale ending that every princess dreams of, the love of her prince charming and a forever and ever.

Chapter XXIV
No resemblance to a fairy tale

One thing is certain, nothing is as it is told, and nothing is as it seems.

When, before getting married, you are told in several medical consultations that you are not going to be able to have children, your greatest desire, the frustration as a female makes you withdraw in a "I am not woman enough?". You question, "why me when I so want to be a mother; why can everyone else but me?" In short, you feel incomplete. But nothing is as we are told, for better or worse. Miracles happen and what is written in our lives, has to happen whether we want it to or not. "If something is not for you, no matter how much you run you will not reach it, but if something is for you, no matter how much you stand still, it will reach you."

The immense joy of knowing the long-awaited news does not exonerate you from what you will have to experience later on. Once again, we find ourselves in the reverie of putting on just the right amount of weight, of looking beautiful, of not suffering any discomfort and of being like the magazine covers. Ha! Not true, at least for me. From joy I went to fear, the cloud of the threat of a miscarriage introduced me into the unpleasant spiral of I don't want to lose my baby, not now. From there to nausea, my close friend was the toilet bowl, from dawn to dusk. There was no pill worth its salt to help me contain it, so the glamour of my magazine cover had become the label of a detergent for bathrooms, "how to disinfect a toilet from the vileness of a constant vomiting". And there is still more, finally, the moment most idealized by rom-coms arrives, the actual moment of childbirth. They do it made up, without dishevelment and with a wonderful smile; but you take a whole day to give birth to your little one, dying of pain until the most exhilarating thing in the world comes at the end. Then the stitches and fever until your milk comes in, in addition to the welcome visitors who arrive at the most unexpected times.

Well, yes, all this, said part in jest, seems like a tremendous drama, but it was always linked to the most important thing, that I didn't care if I was upset, if I was nauseous, if I gave birth looking terrible, because what I loved the most in this world was already in my arms. The purest and most selfless love was going to start giving me the most immense joys, as well as hundreds of sleepless nights in Toledo, trying to turn her desperate crying into a smile.

Life is like that, miraculous, in those moments, even now, I could look at it in a thousand ways, the pragmatic and realistic, the romantic, the sensitive, the sentimental, the emotional, any of them equally worthy, but I decided to see life my way, passionately alive and giving thanks for every little moment, truly the most beautiful of my life, when seen with hindsight.

But that intensity of emotions was, at the same time, both good and not so good. And the excessive sensitivity made me realize that what I was experiencing as a fairy tale was not really so, because, although I fervently wished it were so, it was not real.

Alberto Cortes said in one of his songs:

...and built, castles in the air in the sun, with cotton clouds, in a place where no one could ever reach using reason... and here ends the story of an idiot who, through the air, like the free air, wanted to fly like the seagulls..., but that's impossible..., isn't it?

Routine, loneliness, carrying a wonderful daughter on my shoulders, ended up making me see that my crystal castle like a princess in a fairy tale, watered with the unconditional presence of my Prince Charming, with a daughter on the cover of a magazine, a wonderful house and two wonderful cars, was breaking into a thousand pieces. None of it was worth it if it did not go hand in hand with a full, real and experiential love felt by both of us.

After six years of marriage and overcoming many crises, I wanted to be a mother again. Again, the same uncertainty and the same fears, although somewhat overlapped, because I already had a daughter. At the same time, seasoned with the sauce of a relationship in decline.

But since women in this state are stubborn bitches, and intuiting that I would have another child, I let my innermost self persuade me that this was the right time, even though I knew that such a decision might not bring good consequences to our relationship.

On the eve of San Juan, a magical night if ever there was one, a constant and shrill little voice tortured me all day long, "it's time to do it". But being at Ana and Manuel's house, everything became more complicated of course, as I had my particular appendage glued to my ass, my little girl.

I let the morning hours pass to prepare for an exciting siesta encounter, and said and done, sensual and virtuous, I languished desperately waiting for David to take notice. But either I had lost all ability to seduce, or our love was lost; either way, managing the necessary strategy for the conquest did not seem to me to be an easy task. I don't think so, they also have headaches, they are tired or they are just going to watch the sport of the day are among the excuses.

When naptime came, I set out to put my baby to sleep, hinting to David to come upstairs with me. As the indicative gestures did not bear fruit, I ended up being very clear.

"David, are you going upstairs to take a nap?"

"No. I'm going to read this hunting magazine."

"You'd better come to bed and rest; tonight will be a long night."

"No, I'm staying here."

My plan had gone up in smoke, but my intuition remained stubborn and unbridled.

"Come on, David, come up," I said, winking, indicating with my neck, making the gesture with my hand. Not even the highway code had that many signs.

"You're really annoying. Don't you get it? I don't feel like sleeping."

"Who said anything about sleeping!" I said huskily, "Come on, okay?"

Once the baby fell asleep, I managed to keep my husband from likewise abandoning himself to the arms of Morpheus. So once my plan was in place, I just had to let it flow. And all said and done, a quick and pleasurable encounter that resulted in the most precious child in the world.

That miracle that is intuition should never be disdained, because it is true that we are witches who, without potions or snake fangs, are able to presage that the time has come. If we let opportunities pass, they do not return, leaving a chapter of life unfinished.

And in that wonderful time, when I became a mother for the second time, I understood that I no longer had a prince charming. I had not been told as a child how to maintain "and they lived happily ever after" day after the day. Those bacteria, routine and not knowing who you are, which seems iniquitous, made us mature towards different levels of consciousness towards each other. Giving us the most abrupt and saddest disagreement, which is none other than the lack of love.

At that point in my life, I felt that I was not enough for my other. How sad is that? But sadder still is not realizing that, in reality, the person for whom you are not enough, is enough for you. Realizing that you yourself have put the obstacle there is a problem that is not solved in your head, rather it is felt inside you. It is a knot inside your stomach that oppresses you and prevents you from being natural, from being yourself, that slowly swallows you up until the day comes when you can't take it anymore. You blame the whole world, if necessary, but in truth, the world is not to blame, it is you yourself who cannot forgive your defects and do not trust in your possibilities. You no longer have the balance between the love of a partner and of your children.

To look yourself in the mirror and see that you are no longer the same as yesterday; your whole life is a movie where the protagonist has lost her magic; you are a caricature of the strong and tough Sara. That day really hurts.

I was learning that I should not blame the rest of my world for my problems, for that was to ignore the lessons that life had prepared for me. Experiences that were more than annoying, they hurt; they were little pinches on the arm that don't injure, but they are vexatious. And the worst thing is that they kept happening. They would not stop until I learned the right thing, even when you don't know what it is. I could not let my complaints of that moment become a habit! It would be cowardly.

Even today, those phrases strike in my memory, "I'm leaving, but I'm staying", "I'll leave everything, but I can't", "I want to feel you, but you won't let me", "give me a loving kiss" met with an answer of "you are very tiresome", "I want those curtains" and "I don't like them", "let's go on a trip just the two of us" with a "it is not necessary."

Nothing is as they say and nothing is as it seems.

Chapter XXV
Being your whole life

A shadow has awakened me. My heart beats two thousand beats per hour and I don't know where I am. The blind is down. I can't see a speck of light, my throat is dry, and I have an awful fear of I don't know what. I crawl around the bed desperately looking for the door, but I only stumble against walls, the anguish is suffocating me, and a choked scream comes out of my mouth,

"Mom!"

"Sara, for God's sake, what are those screams!"

"Mom, I didn't know where I was, I woke up screaming and with a knot still choking me."

"Come on, come on, get up and take a shower, you'll see how much better you'll feel afterwards."

After the shower, everything seems normal. I'm at my parents' house. I'm sure the coffee is in tune with me and I'm able to breathe, this heart of mine still wants to escape my body. What an unpleasant feeling.

With a coffee in my hands, I go to the living room. It is Holy Saturday, and my parents are praying. I envy their faith. There is always peace when I enter that wide room, its light dimmed by the white curtains, the characteristic smell of my childhood, the pictures that remind me of moments when I thought "what will become of me", like now. I burst into tears that do not cease and are accentuated in each sorrow.

"Sara, what's wrong?"

"I can't take it anymore, Mom."

"You should have done it a long time ago. It's all right, we're here."

"Did you know what's wrong with me?"

"We have known it for a long time."

That's how it was, no more preambles, no more stories, no more excuses. A single sentence and it changed my life forever. In that absurd way, I was able to make the saddest, if not the hardest decision of my life. From that moment on, the chain of events, some cruel and the rest even more inhuman, began to unleash, resulting in my broken heart.

I did not understand in those moments what life was giving me. I only saw my sorrow. My head was a carousel of unanswered questions and I felt like a failure. I was not capable of loving anymore. I did not understand why I was not loved or, better said, why I did not feel like a loved wife. Was I selfish, insensible, absurd? Was it just me? There are no guilty parties in love stories, there are only events that, without causing us sudden death, kill us little by little. But I did not want to continue agonizing, I had to find my strength, my inner light, that joy that had always accompanied me, I had stopped being myself, I had ceased to look at myself because I no longer liked what I saw. Loneliness.

The worst loneliness, the accompanied loneliness, in which not a moment is for you, in which when you turn off the light, you only want to sleep so that the new day gives way to another, with no greater desire than the hope that everything will change, to feel love.

And why did I have to feel that love? I had been by his side for fifteen years, but we were on separate continents. Holding his hand yet a thousand miles away from him. The pain of knowing that you have put your life, and the other person his, at the disposal of the heart and to then wake up to the hardest reality, that truth which blows up inside you and forces you to put on false smiles when others ask you about your life. You have to show the Sofia Loren that we all carry inside, made up, dressed in your best clothes and wearing heels that separate you from the warmth of the earth, but does not come from the reality of your heart.

Yes, now I understand it with blinding clarity. I am them, in my person, in my blood, in their way of loving; a way in which everything is given to receive everything; in which the embrace and presence is dressed in pure love; in which there is the most imperious need to be there for the other their whole life. And does that make me a better or worse person? Not at all, it only makes us different, two acrobats on parallel ropes of love whose hands never got to hold each other. So much effort to fall into the net of being able to be alone; of having to learn to love yourself because you already know, accept and suffer from being uninhabited.

"David, we need to talk."

"What's wrong?"

"I'm not happy. I think we need to give ourselves some time."

"What's brought this on?"

"That you do not love me, and I do not love you."

"Is that reason enough?"

"I don't know, but I can't live like this."

And is it? Having children, house, work. For me yes, I did not know why I needed to feel included in his whole life, not just a part of it. I did not know why it hurt so much not to be one and to only be his fourth or fifth priority, but I that's how I felt. I was equally aware of the unhappiness in both of us.

And the fact is that, like Ana, I cannot let the pragmatic supplant my feelings, nor do I want to, because it is at that point where I stop being Sara, and to be what others want. Then, Angela comes out of my heart to take a train to my own destiny, but in this case, there could not be a "I love you" postponed like Samuel's, which means that the chain of women loved by men who would give their lives for them is definitely broken.

"Sara, are you sure?"

"David, there is never complete certainty in anything we decide to do. I cannot express what I really feel, but I am certain that this is not healthy, it is not pure, it is not that love for life."

"What do you really need?"

"To be truly important to you."

"Sara, you are. The only thing is that sometimes I can't, or you demand too much."

"I don't feel it is. We live in completely antagonistic worlds. I'm looking for the last moment in which the joy of a simple look made me feel special. There isn't one, David. We have become accustomed to living on tiptoe, without striving to make ourselves happy. The fault was not the work, nor the times, nor the children, it is only ours. I thought I could bear it all my life, how ironic, to endure! I am not capable; my inner self does not let me. It does not allow me to continue wasting more life, because, David, my dear, that is what hurts me the most, to see how we waste the time that life gives us when we are no longer capable of loving each other."

"But I don't feel it like you do, I'm fine like this."

"That is what differentiates us and makes us incompatible. My life must be squeezed to the last drop. I do not want to leave aside either suffering or love. I cannot ignore the fact that I am alive, and I want to drink every drop of existence that is given me. On the contrary, you live comfortably in a constant pulse without searching for what is most intimate. That is not being more coherent than me, or me being braver than you. It is to be attached to our way of being and not to do more harm to the other believing that we are both going to change. I expect from you to be the sun of every day and, at night, to be the passion of your skin. You, on the other hand, only hope that we don't argue, and we can live in peace, stay healthy and work. It's over, David, it's for the best."

No voices, no more reproaches. No war, and no sound to incite it. There was nothing, that's it. End what has been your life and it provokes nothing. A slam of the door, a scream, a thought. There is nothing more.

How indifference and silence break you!

And that's how my desert began. I didn't really know if I was right or not, because it was all too difficult, but there was still the hardest part.

"Sara, I need to talk to you."

"Mom, tell me."

"I wanted to talk last night, but I had your brothers and dad there."

"Don't scare me. Please let me know what's going on."

"Sara, I have cancer."

"What? Wait, I'm going to park the car, I'm on my way down to work."

"Sara, I'm fine, don't hurry and drive calmly."

"Mom, how can I be calm with what you just told me? Are you absolutely sure? Is it a definitive diagnosis? I thought you were going to have a CAT scan."

"Sara, this time it's coming for me. I want you to fix everything before the operation. I want you to have the papers in court and I want you to fight for your children. You are my daughter and I know how mature you are."

"You're breaking me, mom, you speak to me with a calmness that scares me, I don't know if you're just being foolish or if you have an uncommon inner strength. The last thing I care about right now is signing an agreement. You are my strength, mom, without you I can't do it."

"If you keep crying, I'll put down the mobile and I'll give you a couple of thumps that will make you stand up. Come on, dry your tears and stick out your chest. Nobody should know your sorrows, others have them worse and continue with their heads held high, you are not going to do any less."

"Mom, what the hell are you."

I think I will never forget her words, not in themselves, but for their content. That is Ana, a woman who never ceases to assert herself, to ponder self-esteem and inner strength.

Within a month, all was said and done, the papers signed in court and the date of the operation. I had lost so much in those times that the only thing that kept me alive were my children and Mom. Soon it would be her eightieth birthday. I, and my family, had to throw her a very special party. But there was no desire, no ideas.

"Dad, we have to prepare for Mom's eightieth birthday party."

"No, daughter, how can you even think of such a thing, when my Ana is so ill."

"What?" I put myself in front of his eyes and claimed like a fierce woman. "You had a big surprise that she prepared with all her love and the money she was squirrelling away for months, so that you wouldn't suspect anything. It is her moment. Besides, let's be clear about one thing: if my mother dies during the operation, this will be our last happy moment; if, as I hope and pray to God with all the strength of my soul, everything goes well, both she and we will smile when we remember it. I will not allow any of this family to take it for granted that grief is the only antidote to the agony we are going through. She, in her simplicity, holds your hand through these moments as she has throughout your lives. Take courage and let's go for it."

"As you say, daughter, I don't know how you can with all that you have going on."

"I can, because I am your daughter and I love you, Daddy."

After fifteen days, everything was a memory forever. I did what I should have done, but how many things could I have done better? And so, I was left broken with pain and searching for a way to understand myself and my life.

Nearly the final chapter:
I am them and part of them

A generational history makes no sense without an epigraph that gives way to the life that follows. The succession of lives that, before mine, make me, Sara, the way I am. Because "this is who I am".

And I am no more or less than I was before I recognized myself in them, but there is a difference in the knowledge of why I act and think in the way that emerges from my innermost being.

Now I know why my heart is so intense and I write feelings which can't be said, because they are so deep inside that to bring them out is to negate their magic, their essence, the material they are made of. They need to stay in me, because if they were misunderstood, they would provoke pain and denial, and I would withdraw back into my shell and they would return to the corner from where they should not have emerged. But if, on the contrary, they escape through the cells of my skin, reaching the most intimate part of another, they can sweep over me like a tsunami that would provoke changes from within those who sense me. It is then when I return to Angela and Ana, to see in them their strength and the generosity that they lavished on their lives which, still, simply for me, were great jewels, where I treasure myself, realizing that not sharing the intensity of love is to deny myself, to deny what I learned through them.

Now I know why I am love and not something else, because I cannot feel from my mind, because I cannot half undress my soul, because swimming and keeping my clothes on was never my forte. That is why I now know that life hurts when you really love, when you shoot without aiming, because the only thing that exists in you is a passion for life, no matter what it costs and no matter what happens. And I understand and accept that I am like that because they taught me to be so; because to be brave in feelings is to cross the Tartarus without fearing that its doors will close behind me, leaving only one way to go. But I can color that path with my soul; I can put it to music with whispers and sighs; I can straighten it with the right attitude, learning from any mistake. Because I have also learned that we never react to the nice and beautiful things that life gives us, because we believe we have the right to obtain them, we do it with the claw that tears the entrails, that is how we grow and we gather our strength as to come out unscathed from our own experience.

And yes, to love is a right that we all have towards each other, the right to feel that breath in our hearts that pushes us to be a better person. But it is no less true that I also have the right to love and embrace myself in every gesture with the humility of knowing that I am human, forgiving myself for my stumbles and defects of character, which being many, are those that fell upon me at birth and those brought forth by experiencing others. I now understand, love and forgive myself after having learned that I have the right to recognize them in myself and accept them, to grow in every second which that blank check that life gives me every day.

And even more, that the right to love me is equally held by others, who strive to understand my stubborn way of perceiving life, my fanciful and overwhelming way of not conforming to what should be this way or that way. Yes, it is true, they have the right to choose whether to let me be in their lives, without any reproach if they do not; without me blaming them for not choosing me; without seeing in them the obligation to accept me, because they do not have any compulsion to do so. They are the mirror of how I am, how I should change and how I should find myself. To understand and accept that if I am not accepted, I am no less Sara; that I cannot be loved by everyone who appears in my present and future; that these are not failures but lessons in which I can recognize myself more and more. Just as Angela was rejected at the dawn of her youth, forced to leave her village to forget, with elegance, humility and pride. It was then that she discovered and cultivated her innermost being to blossom into the humble lady that during her short life she was able to radiate. Like my beloved mother, she was able to adapt to the most adverse circumstances to assert herself and teach her beloved son, Manuel, what she was like, without concealment, transparent and faithful to her being.

But it is also true that, through them, as a spur and on the pyramid of their lives, I have understood that I have the right to say no. No to what is not part of me; no to what I do not share; no to what I do not feel; no to what does not make me happy. I have the right and, this time, the obligation to defend the only thing that is really mine, me. But to do it from the most exquisite sweetness, because you should not offend gratuitously, because offending not only hurts the offended, it hurts you as well, when you see that the worst part of you emerges when it least should and regret arises, feeling like trash but at your own hands. No, and a thousand times no, to that part that we all innately carry, because yes, we all have that binomial that makes us shine and give the best of ourselves, as well as that latent evil that counterbalances our good deeds; a perverse side that should remain dormant in the Pandora's box that we carry on our backs.

And that treasured love in my heart. I am aware that I did not live it with the intensity that they experienced in their lives. And I did not do it for lack of desire or because I was not loved, but because life has made me understand what love between a man and a woman really is. Throughout the experiential search of my family history, I have discovered that this visceral passion of the essence of love, this wanting everything for everything, makes me indefatigable in the search of the encounter, of sharing, of adding and never subtracting, of intuiting what is needed and desired, of being with you and not without you, of dying because I lose you and living because I love you and you love me. It is true, each one of us loves in our own way and in the way we have learned. And I have conformed to the best teachers. I have felt that full love that, only on certain occasions and with certain people, life gives us. And why not to me? Because life is wise, it teaches you its lure until you see yourself worthy and capable of feeling what love should really be. And then you learn that there are people who make the path and others who live the results, that there are women who sow the seed and generations to come who enjoy the fruits.

I have yet to discover whether it was my turn to sow or to reap, but either way, I know that I want to love and listen to Puccini in my heart, but in the meantime, I have realized that I am a full orange that only needs to be watered and cared for so that its fragrance, flavor, texture and sweetness will be even better.

To be loved in every exact moment of life, to feel that you are able to give life and to do it from the most perfect, pleasant and exciting place, that of being a mother. The most recondite illusion of all the determined ones, to know that, in that narrow and small place, the life of my children made a way for me to go with them for the rest of my days.

Some say that it is a mortgage for life, because I want to get into debt up to my eyebrows in this loan of love that God gave me. I want to do it forever and ever in the commitment of "I will love you and take care of you for life", because I had not felt Ana's love, in its most just measure, until I had my little one. It was then when I discovered the immensity and infinity of her love. The patience in the protective care that makes even the air that touches them bother you. The smell of their bodies, part of your blood and your cells, which prolongs your being to two other beings to raise and educate, when they are the ones who with their coming make you grow in every way; when they are the ones who make you get up from any nonsense; when they are the engine of each and every one of the days that make up the rest of your life.

And it could not be otherwise. Once again Angela and Ana, coexist in my maternal being, predestine me to the need to be a mother and extend that love in my lineage, that generosity of mother's love that drop by drop of milk and with infinite patience was able to bring me to life and make this Sara a woman who became a mother. Thank you, and a thousand thanks, for coming to this saga of women who before me were in all their essence and fullness.

Although it may seem contradictory, I, Sara, have also discovered that, in the way of being love, I give myself to others and I am independent. And yes, I am. Many people who read these lines will be comforted knowing that they recognize themselves in them. Because being true, I give myself body and soul to my loved ones, putting them before my needs. It is no less true that I am a free and independent spirit, who finds it hard to ask for help, because I believe I'm capable, with will and courage, of anything to which life itself may expose me. But this rootedness and bravery is not my genetic inheritance from Angela and Ana -even though they both were in their lives- but, in this case, it was Samuel and Manuel who opened the path of effort and dedication, of the need to cultivate the being from the work that dignifies and solitude itself. Both left their lives grateful for forging a better future, or perhaps simply a different one. They fought against titans and dragons, wounds of war and of the soul, but they remained there empowering their most intimate strength in the freedom and independence granted to them by their condition as men.

And this time I, Sara, the youngest of this family saga, breaks the social conditioning to know and find herself in the skin of an independent and shrewd woman who bites the overwhelming clutches of fate, taking out that courageous woman that sometimes also has to gore life itself, splinting her own heart to keep beating strongly.

Perhaps, as they say in my land, "if it were a farmhouse, it would be in no man's land", because that brave nature that I feel, sometimes makes me unable to assimilate anything that does not come from the well of wisdom that gives experience, sometimes external, but almost always my own. And I declare myself irreverent, because I do not understand any act that does not come from the influence of vital causalities, in which I choose, like them, to be a protagonist in the theater of life and not a mere spectator.

We all have that masculine and feminine essence that makes us special and different from the rest of creation. Blessed humanity that made us rational and gave us the strength to be complete and in fullness to be men and women.

And in that complete identity where my woman's soul sails on its heels to know that I am free and capable, the lyrics of a song assaults me, as so often:

It won't be easy to be one heart again. I had always been one half without knowing my identity. I will not carry any image from here, I will leave naked just as I was born. I must begin to be myself and know that I am capable and that I walk by my skin....

From my freedom, by Ana Belén.

It is true. I, Sara, am able to live my own life, this time consistent with my "now", perpetuating my history and thirst for the future, for my future. I am able to give it the colors and nuances that each day offers me in its undeniable freshness, the unknown, and in the magnitude of its seconds, as well as the magic and spell that it gives me.

I, Sara, am happy to conceive myself alive and ready to experience all the good, and less good, that every moment brings to me, knowing that from mistakes, I learn, and from caresses, I bask and extract the pleasure that comes from recognizing myself in the fullness of my maturity.

I, Sara, accept that I am my own story; and the one I have yet to write; always being fully aware that "everything is fine as it is", because in that true balance I can always be myself, without forgetting that the protagonist of all the stories I have lived is me, Cruz Galdón, and because "I am them".